Lovesome

T0347558

Lovesome

Sally Seltmann

ALLEN&UNWIN
SYDNEY • MELBOURNE • AUCKLAND • LONDON

First published in 2018

Allen & Unwin
83 Alexander Street
Crows Nest NSW 2065
Australia
Phone: (61 2) 8425 0100
Email: info@allenandunwin.com
Web: www.allenandunwin.com

 A catalogue record for this book is available from the National Library of Australia

ISBN 978 1 76063 287 8

Set in 12/17 pt Fairfield Light by Post Pre-press Group, Brisbane
Printed and bound in Australia by Griffin Press

10 9 8 7 6 5 4 3 2

The paper in this book is FSC® certified. FSC® promotes environmentally responsible, socially beneficial and economically viable management of the world's forests.

For Darren and Judy

1

I have a collection of photographs stored inside my mind. All very detailed. Portraits, group shots, exteriors, interiors, décor and everything. They're predictions of how I imagine the big milestones in my life might turn out. Riding in to work tonight I ponder my most recent mishap, comparing it to my very different pre-imagined version. As I'm doing this I pass the small weatherboard houses and take a left turn onto Darling Street. I continue on, gazing over at a well-dressed couple walking along, arm in arm. The air of contentment that floats between them is a bit much for me to handle this evening, so I pedal harder as huge wafts of laughter, broken beats and cigarette smoke drift out onto the road from the Emerald. My local. It's cold and wintery, so I'm scarfed up, and have somehow managed to fit my black beret under my bike helmet. I dip down the hill, feeling the icy breeze on my face and the rush of adrenaline as I pick up speed, rolling along beside the parked cars. All the warm yellow glowing windows of the sandstone cottages flash past me, until I come to the section of my journey that I lovingly refer to as 'the valley'. I keep riding on the flat black bitumen road as fast as I can, lifting my bum up off the seat as I approach the hill, then pedal my heart out. I know I'm nearly there when I catch my usual glimpse of the harbour. The reflected night lights flicker on the water's surface as though tiny coloured jewels and diamonds are being tossed around in a black blanket.

Out of breath and feeling truly invigorated, I hop off my second-hand ladies' bike and wheel it up the sandstone gutter on the left-hand side of the road. I feel my chest rise and fall as I look beyond the white picket fence at Harland. Looks like someone's hung a new wreath on its front door. I wheel my bike towards the side gate, admiring the twisted, overgrown wisteria vine that climbs up the columns supporting the awning over its small front verandah. Being winter, the vine is bare, with no leaves or grape-like flowers, but I love the tangled patterns of the wooden stems just as much as when the vine is in full bloom.

I keep heading down the side path, then lean my bike against the wall of the shed next to the little outhouse toilet. Unfastening the clasp of my bike helmet and latching it onto one of the handlebars, I hear my silver bell give a slight tinkle, and I can't help smiling. I stuff my hair underneath my beret, and climb the rickety wooden stairs. Looking down beyond my black-and-blue floral dress, I note the variegated pattern of dark green moss on the sandstone step at the top. My hand-knitted black cardigan, under a blue denim jacket, is hardly enough to keep me warm in this weather, but I liked the look when I stood in front of my full-length mirror fifteen minutes ago, so I went with it. I open the broken screen door, then push the heavy, dark-brown worn-looking door behind it with my shoulder. Walking in through the back entrance I can smell the regular mix of chicken and veal, vegetables and parsley, pastry and butter. The heat from the log fire warms my cheeks, and the empty chairs tucked under tables fill me with a sense of excitement. I love the calm before the storm.

Six months ago I found an advertisement in the hospitality column of the jobs section in the Saturday paper: *Waitress Wanted for French Restaurant in Balmain East*. After my trial run one busy Friday night, I was given the job. Five nights a week, starting around six, knocking off between eleven and midnight, and Tuesday and Thursday nights were to be my nights off. A few weeks later I moved out of my share house in Ultimo, and into my current place, meaning my travel time to work is now only about ten minutes.

'Hi Dave,' I say, smiling, as I poke my head into the kitchen.

'Joni! You're early! How was your day?'

'Okay.'

'Only okay? I'll come and have a coffee with you.'

Dave has an enthusiastic bounce to his step. He walks out of the kitchen into the little bar area, where a coffee machine sits alongside bottles of wine and liquor.

'Latte?' he asks.

'Yes please.'

Dave's apron hangs low around his tiny hips, its tie in a loose bow over his baggy chequered chef pants. I sit in my favourite spot, in the cosy back corner of the staff table beside the floor lamp, so I can take in everything that's going on. I always feel relaxed and at home at Harland. I'm comforted by the vintage furnishings, the mismatched china plates, the cat Tiger-Lily, who lives in the back garden. There's a romantic and free-spirited energy that fills the place. Everything's a little old-world and worn-out, in a nostalgic kind of way. Harland really is quite magical.

I sometimes imagine what it must have looked like before it was converted into a restaurant. The stand-alone, double-fronted weatherboard house with sandstone bricks at the bottom. So typical of the Balmain area. Lucy told me that the Red Room, Gatsby and Lillibon used to be the three main bedrooms in the house. They are now set up with old cedar dining tables and chairs. The lounge room and bathroom were converted into what is now the kitchen. I'm guessing this all would have happened about fifteen years ago, in the early 1980s, just before Harland started operating as a restaurant. The Bar Room and staff table, where I'm sitting now, was probably once the second lounge room, or the children's play room.

'What's been happening today?' Dave tilts his head, speaking loudly over the sound of milk being frothed in the stainless-steel jug.

I pause until I see him pouring the warm white liquid into the glass tumbler. I know I should tell him straight away, but it's too awkward, so I offer up small talk.

'I've been working on that painting I was telling you about last night. Just playing around with how abstract I want to go. I'm using oils, hence my hands this evening.' I hold up my right hand, revealing my vermilion palm. 'I know Lucy hates it when I don't get the paint off my hands properly. I did try, but I was in a rush 'cause I thought I'd be late.'

I reach into my bag and fossick around for the rose hand cream I carry with me. Rubbing it in, I continue.

'It's for that group show I was telling you about. I'm so excited! Can't wait. I feel like I'm really getting there, Dave. New theme, new direction. It's strong, I know it is. And it's a great bunch of artists I'll be exhibiting with.'

'So you've found yourself. I thought you would,' Dave says to me, turning his head as he continues to make his coffee.

'I knew it would be hard for me to say goodbye to art school.'

Dave turns towards me. 'But you knew you'd eventually get back on track. Yeah?'

When I first started working at Harland, I was in the midst of hanging my works for the opening of 'Blue Lights', the graduation exhibition at my art school. This was when I'd first met Dave and Lucy and Juliet, and the other Harland staff. Once the exhibition was over and I'd officially graduated, I felt relieved that I had Harland as a place to go, be busy, earn money, talk, analyse things. And now with Annabelle having been away in London for a few months, my world really does revolve around Harland. It's kind of like a second home.

Dave leaves the coffee machine with his espresso and my latte. He joins me in the corner, handing me my freshly made coffee.

'Thanks,' I say.

I slowly wrap my paint-stained palms around the warm glass and look down at the little star tattoo on the inside of my wrist. Bringing the cup to my lips, the aroma of the coffee and the rose hand cream are in conflict with each other. I look Dave in the eyes. I can't hold it in any longer.

'I need to tell you about last night,' I say.

'What?'

'Big mistake!' I wince, unlocking my eyes from Dave's, and lowering my gaze. 'Really big mistake!'

'What?' Dave asks again, smiling.

I turn to see Lucy walking into the room. Her blonde hair is swept up loosely, held together with gold hair combs, and she has flowers pinned above her left ear. She wears a red velvet dress that's low-cut and revealing, and the gold rings on her fingers catch the light. I can smell her musky perfume.

'Tell you later,' I say quickly to Dave.

Lucy's carrying a pile of freshly washed and ironed white tablecloths. She's busy, as always, and moves about quickly with a gorgeous bohemian swiftness that is mesmerising.

'Hey Joni.' She smiles. 'I'm running behind tonight—do you mind setting up the Pines? It needs to be set for six people.' She puts the pile of tablecloths neatly on the shelf below the bar, leaving one of them draped over her arm. I watch her closely, wishing I had a French accent like hers.

'I've already put all the cutlery and plates on the sideboard down there. Thanks, my love,' she tells me sharply, her tone of voice cancelling out the thanks.

I leave my coffee on the staff table, take the damask cloth from Lucy and walk briskly out the back door, down the stairs and along the winding path. The Pines is a smaller cottage in the back garden, separate from the main house, but still part of Harland. I imagine it would have been used as a granny flat, back in the days when Harland was a family home.

I have a love/hate relationship with the walk from the back door of Harland down the path to the Pines. I'm almost certain there are ghosts here. The youngest daughter of the family who occupied the house in the 1950s? Maybe. Did she die a tragic death in her teenage years, and is she here, haunting all the Harland staff? Or is it one of the other children who may have lived in the house? Maybe at the turn of the century?

My imagination runs wild. I hear whispers, and I say to myself, *Don't see a ghost, don't see a ghost*, as if that will somehow ward off any supernatural activity. Even though I don't think I really believe in ghosts. If it's not ghosts, then there's definitely someone in the bushes watching me every time I walk this path, I swear! I don't know why Lucy has never arranged to have the path lit properly.

I set up the table in the Pines. As I'm arranging the wine glasses, I hear Dave calling me from the back door. 'Joni, dinner's up!'

I walk as fast as I can back up that haunted path, feeling the swish of my dress between my legs, hearing my breath quicken.

Juliet has arrived, and is sitting at the staff table. 'Hey Joni,' she says.

She sits confidently, splayed out, her upper body flopped over the wooden table as she whinges about the resin jewellery she was working on today. The moulds were disastrous; the resin did not set; the movie she saw this afternoon was rubbish. Juliet talks a lot. Complains often. Possibly more than anyone I've ever met.

Her skin is pale and slightly freckled, and her light brown hair looks as if it's trying to be red but hasn't quite got there. Her face resembles a full moon, and her small button nose is possibly her most attractive facial feature. Her almost-not-there eyebrows arch above her light brown eyes, and she's kinda short. Shorter than me, and shorter than Lucy.

I hate the cheap-looking cream crocheted vest she's wearing tonight, wrapped over her long denim dress. But I would never dare tell her that. Her silver chain earrings are horribly unfashionable, and her black patent leather shoes look wrong with her dress. I know I'm being judgemental, but I can't help it.

'*Blanquette de veau*, ladies,' says Dave, exiting the kitchen carrying two white bowls, each with steam dancing above the rim. He places them on the table, wanders back into the kitchen, and returns with another bowl. 'Vegies and rice for you, Joni. Is that cool?'

I'm the only vegetarian at Harland. Lucy always pays me out about it, but Dave happily puts a meal together for me every night, and hasn't complained once.

'Hi Joni! Hi Juliet!' Michael calls from the kitchen. He's the other chef at Harland, kind of Dave's assistant. He keeps to himself and never really talks to me.

Lucy flies down the hallway towards the Bar Room and grabs a bottle from the fridge under the bench. 'Little treat tonight, girls.' She pulls down three glasses and pours Juliet, me and herself a splash of chablis to have with our staff dinner.

As always, Lucy doesn't sit to eat hers. She has a mouthful, answers the phone, takes a booking, has another mouthful, clears a bench. She can't sit still, that woman. She's so suited to running a place like this.

Juliet and I remain seated, eating, while Lucy reads from the large book that sits below the phone on the wall. 'We've got a six in the Red Room, three twos and a four in Gatsby, and an eight in Lillibon.'

'And a six in the Pines!' I shout out through a mouthful of peas.

'Is that set?' asks Lucy, retouching her red lipstick while looking at her reflection in the silver coffee machine.

'Yep,' I confirm.

'Okay, Joni, you're taking care of Gatsby and the Red Room. Juliet, you're in Lillibon and the Pines. I'll float between rooms.'

I love how all the rooms in Harland have a name.

'Yay, the Pines,' says Juliet.

'Shit, it's nearly six-thirty!' Lucy announces, stuffing one last forkful into her mouth, then taking her plate into the kitchen.

'Where's Simon?' she calls out.

'Dishies are always late,' I hear Dave saying, just as Simon walks through the back door.

'I heard that. Here I am,' he says, sounding more relaxed than the average person, which of course makes me think he's been out the back smoking a joint and listening to our conversation for the last five minutes.

'Simey!' says Dave, and gives him a half slap-half hug on the back. Simon grabs an apron from the hook near the entrance to the kitchen.

Juliet and I look at each other and smile, while Lucy turns up *Best of Billie Holiday* on the CD player, which we've heard a thousand times.

I hear the sound of the bells, signalling the opening of the front door. Peeking down the hallway I spy a middle-aged couple. I grab my black apron off the hook, slipping into it as fast as I can.

'Girls, we're on,' says Lucy, as she glides towards the front door. '*Bonsoir*. Welcome to Harland,' she smiles.

2

I leave my black beret on the hatstand on top of my cardigan and jacket. Then I do a Lucy, and check my reflection in the side of the coffee machine. My long brown hair looks free and loose and messy—exactly how I like it. Lucy walks briskly back into the Bar Room to check the bookings diary and see where the couple are to be seated.

'Joni, tidy your hair and seat them on table two in Gatsby,' she orders in an overbearing tone, bordering on rude.

She takes a sip of her wine and light-heartedly taps me on the shoulder with two menus. I take them from her, breathing in deeply. I reluctantly smooth my hair with my free hand, catching another glimpse of myself in the Art Deco mirror as I walk along the hallway, readying myself for the night ahead.

Lucy is like a bossy governess. A commander-in-chief, with a paradoxically flippant nature. There's an alluring charm to the playful, yet firm, way she hands out orders. Sometimes she makes out that she's on the same level as us employees, and at other times she shocks us with her authoritarian commands. She's vivacious, with a perfect slender figure and flawless olive skin. Her large almond-shaped hazel eyes have a fierceness that's quite intimidating; I can tell that she was the rebellious kid at school, who got away with everything and still scored high grades. She looks like a young Brigitte Bardot; and when she's having her coffee break out the back, smoking a cigarette, she looks more like a Hollywood starlet than a restaurant owner. I'm certain it's one of the reasons that Harland is almost always booked to capacity.

I was intrigued when I first learnt that Lucy's parents died tragically in a car accident, about ten years ago. She's never told me this herself, but Dave filled me in one night. He said Lucy grew up in Paris, and her parents were furniture dealers. Furniture dealers who had a lot of money. I guess, born into it. Apparently Lucy moved to Sydney about ten years ago; shortly afterwards, her parents visited her here, and then . . . the accident. Dave said it made the nightly news and the front page of the papers. In April 1985, I think he said. A dark filmic image of a smashed car wrapped around a telephone pole on a country road comes to mind when I think back to how Dave described the scene of the tragedy. It's like Australiana meets Hitchcock, my version. The headlights are still on, smoke is rising slowly out of the crushed bonnet, and the branches of the gum trees that line the road are lit up from below.

It was late one evening, and Lucy's parents had been out at a dinner party. Her father was well over the limit when their car slid off the road and hit the wooden pole. Both died instantly. Lucy was an only child, so all their money went to her. Dave said Harland saved her. If she hadn't had the restaurant up and running at that time, she would have collapsed in a heap and suffered a major nervous breakdown. (Dave's words, not mine.)

Lucy never talks about her parents, their death, or anything related to them. To me this seems really weird. I'm certain I'd need to debrief on a regular basis my thoughts and emotions on being parentless. Lucy's reluctance to talk about her past is just another sign of how tough and fearless she is. That's what I think, anyway. She's fiery, fiercely independent, feminine and flirtatious. The four Fs.

I grab my notebook, a pen and a bottle opener from the antique sideboard in the hall, opposite the Art Deco mirror. I slip them into the front pocket of my apron.

'Good evening,' I say to the couple Lucy left waiting in the entrance hall. 'Your table is this way.' I lead them to the best table for two in the house.

It's tucked in the front left-hand corner of Gatsby. A small fire burns in the ornate fireplace almost opposite their table, the orange and yellow flames swaying to and fro at their own will, giving a homely feel to the room. A framed oil painting hangs above the fireplace. I've critiqued it many times: too much brown, the rocks protruding from the cliff face look flat and two-dimensional, the canvas is too small for the subject matter. I can hear Mr Rogers in first-year Painting, asking the class in his hilarious faux English accent: 'Does the painting generate an emotional response from you? What is the mood? Does the mood suit the subject matter?'

The woman looks around and murmurs, 'Oh, lovely,' bringing me back into the room.

I pull both chairs out from the table, and lay the menus on the damask tablecloth, in between the mismatched silver-plated

French cutlery. I unfold the pressed white napkins and place them on the couple's laps, keeping my paint-stained palms faced inward at all times.

'Can I get you a drink to start with?' I ask, with a lilting inflection.

The woman draws a bottle of wine from her oversized maroon leather handbag.

'Are you BYO?' she asks.

'Yes,' I tell her.

She hands me the wine bottle, and I attempt to open it in front of them with the bottle opener. The cork is in so tight, and I unfortunately screw the opener in crooked. Damn! I can't get the cork out! I pull an awkward face and bend my knees, gripping the bottle between my legs. I notice Lucy walking in to check on me; she shakes her head like a strict headmistress, making me feel like a complete fool. I straighten up hastily, removing the bottle from between my legs.

Lucy comes up behind me and yanks the bottle from my hands. She pulls the cork out in one swift manoeuvre, then passes the bottle back to me and walks away.

The woman at the table smiles. 'Wow, that was impressive!' she says, watching Lucy walk out of the room. She turns her face back towards me. 'What a gorgeous dress.'

'Thanks,' I say.

'Oh no, I mean the other lady's dress,' she says, making me feel extremely embarrassed.

'I remember her from last time,' the man tells her, confirming my belief that people only dine here because they have the hots for Lucy.

I, on the other hand, am a forgettable twenty-one-year-old

nobody. I remember serving this couple a few months ago. But of course they don't remember me. They only remember Lucy.

As I pour a glass of wine for each of them, I'm taken to a dreary corner in my mind where a Super 8 film is playing my least favourite childhood memory. The clickety-clack of the projector provides the soundtrack to Kitty Grayson in the school playground, teasing me. She's saying, in her thin, ugly voice, that I'll grow old alone and no man will ever love me. The memory haunts me to this day.

I shuffle back towards the Bar Room, my self-esteem deflating rhythmically with every step. I expect to be roused on by Lucy, but it's only Juliet I find, seated at the table, finishing her meal. She's humming 'Smells Like Teen Spirit', and she sounds like a pre-pubescent choirboy with a blocked nose. It's nauseating. Annabelle would call it sacrilege. I look through the Victorian windows and see Lucy sitting on the back verandah with her wine glass in hand and a red-and-black chequered mohair rug around her shoulders. She exhales a huge puff of smoke towards the stars; then she looks me right in the eyes and shakes her head. She chuckles, and once again I'm reminded that she's constantly amused by my incompetent waitressing.

Dave pokes his head out of the kitchen. His cheeks are red from the heat of the stove and his skin is a little shiny. Tonight he wears his shoulder-length mousey brown hair pulled back in a tight ponytail, a few loose strands falling in front of his small blue eyes.

'I still want to know what happened last night,' he says with a grin.

'I know,' I say quietly, the sting of my failed bottle-opening attempt easing. 'Later, later. You hanging around for a knock-off drink tonight?'

'Am I hanging around? Joni J, I always stay for a drink!'

I walk into the kitchen and get close to him so no one else can hear.

'Well, I need to get you alone to tell you, okay? I don't want Lucy and everyone else listening in. I'll try to clear the Pines, or reset it or something. Let's talk when I'm down there, and I'll tell you about it all.'

'Gotcha.' Dave throws the greasy tea towel over his shoulder and gives me a wink.

The reason I want to confide in Dave is because he's such a good listener. And I value his advice. Plus, he brings a funny slant to anything and everything I tell him, so I know he'll help me to lighten up about the whole thing.

I've gotten to know Dave well since I started working at Harland. We're good friends, whereas all the other staff members feel more like co-workers and not really close buddies. I've learnt all sorts of things about Dave, like how he was the state champion in high jump in 1988, which to me is quite surprising, mainly because he isn't very tall. But I guess he has the ability to bounce up and rise above things, making the whole high jump win a fitting metaphor for his disposition.

Dave's mum brought him up on her own. Him and his brother Jake, who is slightly younger and uglier. When I met Jake, he was standing beside Dave and it made me realise that Dave is actually pretty good-looking. And their mum—Dave tells me—is amazing. A glass-half-full woman, who left their dad when Dave was two, and brought them up while studying at uni part-time.

'A very bad decision' is how his mum describes Dave's biological father. But she made life fun—always—which cancelled out Dave's desire to have a father present in his life. Plus, Dave got the glass-half-full gene. Glass-two-thirds-full, actually.

After I leave Dave to get back to it in the kitchen, I tidy up the staff table, and give it a good wipe over with a cloth. As I do this I'm reminded of the time Dave told me—when we were all talking about religion and beliefs—that life should be about learning, having meaningful friendships, and enjoying yourself. From my point of view, he's constantly putting his own personal motto into practice. And he does it with an effortless grace. A blokey sort of grace that draws people in.

I think it was his mum who taught him how to live like this, just from the way he's described her. And I can see that Dave's admiration for his mother's academic achievements, and the way she raised two happy, motivated boys on a single income, is what inspires him to keep the learning/friendship/enjoy yourself doctrine alive.

I like Dave. Very much. He's into so many things that I'm into, and he has a real appreciation for the arts. He even loves *Breathless* by Jean-Luc Godard as much as I do.

But we only have a brother/sister kind of thing going on. I think.

3

Juliet and I greet more couples and groups as they come through the front door of Harland. We seat them and we serve them, while Lucy flits around criticising our service skills, throwing witty jokes at the boys in the kitchen, and smoking cigarettes out the back. Lillibon and the Red Room also have small fireplaces, and Lucy keeps an eye on them throughout the evening. She stokes them with ornate brass pokers, and adds more firewood when needed.

The best-looking fireplace is in the Red Room, and it's also the only room in Harland with dark caramel-coloured wood panelling on all the walls. It gives it a folksy, second-hand-store feel. There's a collection of red vases on the mantelpiece, which Dave told me once belonged to Lucy's parents. Larger red urns and vases from the collection also sit on the high shelf that runs along the wall of this room, opposite the doorway.

Below the medley of larger urns and vases hang three framed prints of black-and-white Harold Cazneaux photographs. They each have the title and year captioned in neat handwriting at the bottom. I like the one on the right best: *Wharfies, Circular Quay* (1910). It features a bunch of men wearing suits and hats leaning against the fence at Circular Quay. Behind them is a ship, or large ferry. A huge cloud of steam rises from what looks like the funnel of a smaller ferry in front. It's a mysterious, painterly fog. I often get lost in this image, imagining what all the men are thinking.

I love it when Lucy gives me the Red Room to take care of. The window looking onto the street is hung with red velvet curtains drawn back with brocade ties. They're so beautiful. At first I thought it was a nod to *Twin Peaks*, the whole Red Room thing, but Lucy told me she set the room up like this five years before *Twin Peaks* was on TV. I think that's bullshit, but I don't dare suggest that she's lying, because she would severely wound me with her sharp words if I ever murmured dissent. She wins every argument she's part of. She's a knife-throwing champion, her cutting remarks capable of leaving permanent scars. Yet there is a side of her I really admire. The interior designer, the 'woman with creative flair', who is capable of creating worlds as glorious as the Red Room.

I mean, all the furnishings and the quirky details. Everything on display stimulates the imagination. When I stand in there taking orders, waiting for someone to choose between the pâté or the soufflé, I look around, taking it all in. The collection of old Valentine's Day cards and ornaments that hang on little gold hooks, framing the door, keeps me entertained during the long pauses I need to endure after asking, 'And what would you like for your entrée?' The black silhouette of a man and a woman inside a red velvet heart is a favourite, even though it's hideously kitsch.

Or I turn to look at the urns and vases on the shelf. I love the ornate Japanese urn with multicoloured leaves wrapped around its bulging sides. And the brighter red glass vase, with its etching in white of a girl sitting in a tree. Her body is twisted, and her elbow rests casually on the branch. Her stillness reminds me of 'Ode on a Grecian Urn' by Keats. Every night she watches me seat the groups of six or eight. She watches me take down the orders on my little notepad. She catches me accidentally spilling gravy, and apologising profusely, as I deliver the meals. The girl on the branch watches my every move. But she doesn't see me when I leave Harland and ride home. When I paint during the day. When I snuggle up in bed on the mezzanine level of my bungalow. Or when I dream of one day having a boyfriend.

Lucy keeps all the firewood outside, stacked in a small shed someone built out of old fence palings. Its corrugated iron roof hangs over a little extra on the left, acting as a shelter for our bikes. It's beside the outhouse toilet, on the left of the path that leads down towards the Pines.

Juliet is supposed to be keeping the fire alive down there tonight. That's the deal when Lucy gives you the Pines as your designated responsibility. You keep the fire burning gently, letting it ease off to hot coals only towards the end of the evening. My guess, though, is that Juliet will completely forget to re-stock the fire tonight, because she has a tendency to overlook at least one of the duties Lucy hands her.

At around nine-fifteen the first couple I served in Gatsby have left, leaving behind a large tip, which I can only assume is for Lucy. I reset their table, in case we get a walk-in, realising I'll need to head down to the Pines to get some clean napkins to complete the setting. Before I brave the cold, I make a quick coffee for myself in the Bar Room. As I froth the milk, I turn and catch Tiger-Lily walking up close to the back window. Poor little tabby cat, out there in the cold. She wants to come in, but she's not allowed to when we're open for business.

I take a few sips of my coffee, and its warm silken rush runs down my throat. I leave it on the bar, knowing I'll be back soon to finish it off. Pushing open the back door, then the screen door, I feel the icy winter air on my face. Down the steps, along the dark path, on my way to the Pines. I tell myself, *Don't see a ghost, don't see a ghost*, until the sound of chitter-chattering and the clink of cutlery on china plates overtakes the mantra inside my head. I see the group of diners through the window, and they're laughing and carrying on in a raucous fashion. A woman dressed in black, with a long bob, gold earrings and a loud voice, appears to be holding court. She sits with her back to the fire, which, as I had predicted, is out. *Finito!*

I creep in and pull back the floral curtain which acts as a door to the storage area. It's like a walk-in wardrobe. Lucy keeps the freshly ironed napkins stacked on a shelf in here, along with some tablecloths, spare wine glasses, coffee beans, silver spoons, sugar . . . a whole range of things. I count out eight napkins, listening in to their heated discussion about who is more likely to have an affair out of all the couples in their group tonight. I can't even imagine what it would feel like to be in a relationship with someone for long enough to be worrying about affairs.

Keeping my head down, I exit the Pines. *Don't see a ghost, don't see a ghost*, I say to myself, hanging on tightly to the napkins. Halfway along the path I raise my head and find I'm about to bump into Juliet. She's leaning over the firewood in the little shed, with a log in each hand.

'It's already out,' I tell her. 'I don't know if you'll be able to light it again unless you take some kindling.'

'Joni, you're always worrying about something,' Juliet says.

'I'm not worried about it, I just don't think you'll be able to get in there behind Loud-Talking Long-Bob.'

She brushes past me. 'I've done this a million times.'

Yes, you've neglected the fire and let it burn out while our customers freeze to death. Many times. Probably not a million times, but at least twenty times.

As Juliet passes me I smell her Fuzzy Peach perfume, a Body Shop fragrance I once thought was cute and fruity, but now despise. Anything on Juliet smells annoying.

'Have no fear—your friendly fire-lighter is here!' I hear her announce, as she walks back into the Pines.

Juliet has her own thing going on, which I give her credit for, but most of the time I find her extremely irritating. She seems to cling to the idea that she's a creative powerhouse, when really I don't think she has a creative bone in her body. Okay, possibly one or two; but I've seen her resin jewellery and it's definitely not quite there yet. She told me once that she dreams of being able to live off selling her resin bangles and earrings, as well as the wooden jewellery boxes she makes with plywood and paints with watercolours.

But she's been developing these products for over a year now and, amid all the complaints and whining, what she's producing does not look like it's anywhere close to becoming something that anyone would want to purchase. She tells me she's already started selling them, but I'm not sure whether to believe this, because she didn't look me in the eye when she said it.

As I wander up the garden path, I remember back to a few months ago, when Dave, Juliet, Lucy and I had shared a round of knock-off drinks up at the Emerald. Juliet somehow managed to corner me and give me a brief summary of her youth.

'My parents ran the Wallaby Arms Hotel in Lismore,' she'd said, in her yelly, broad Australian accent. 'They still do. We lived upstairs, growing up, you know? And all the kids in our neighbourhood thought I was so cool, because Mum and Dad ran the classiest pub in the area.'

Dave later told me this wasn't really true. He did a road trip to Byron Bay with Lucy and Juliet last year, and they'd dropped in to Juliet's home town. Dave said the pub had an exterior paint job that screamed Shocking Colour Scheme. In the bistro the tables and chairs were white plastic, with grubby grey scratches all over them, and there were clear plastic tablecloths, if that's what you'd call them. Dave said that despite this, the interior was pretty cool and relaxed, but definitely not 'classy'. He told me that the whole pub stank of sweaty men in singlets, mixed with the whiff of stale beer that rose like steam from the forty-year-old carpet. Meanwhile, across the road from the basic establishment run by Juliet's parents, stood what was very obviously the real Classiest Pub in Lismore.

But Dave did say that Juliet's parents were hilarious and he and Lucy were in stitches taking part in their nightly story-telling sessions. Dave said he totally saw where Juliet gets her funny streak from.

'I have three brothers,' Juliet continued as she told me her back story at the Emerald. 'They all live in Brisbane. All married with kids, and all successful businessmen. But I'm the white sheep, and I always have been.'

She probably meant black sheep, but I couldn't be bothered correcting her.

'And I'm the creative one in the family. By the way,' she said, while her spit made it onto my lip, 'I'm named after Shakespeare's *Romeo and Juliet*. You know, the play?'

Of course I knew, but I gave her a fake *I think so* look, hoping her story would eventually come to an end.

'So yeah, I'm like the literary, arty one,' she said, proudly sticking her boobs out, and flicking her hair out of her eyes. She took a slug of her chardonnay, during which time I managed to squeeze out of the corner and over to Dave, where I told him, 'I find Juliet a bit annoying.'

And in true Dave style he said, 'She's alright. She's alright.'

He sees the best in everyone.

I push open the back door of Harland and return to my coffee on the bar, after resting the pile of napkins on a clear section of the staff table. I savour my last sip, knowing it will give me an extra burst of energy as I start taking dessert orders in the Red Room.

'Everybody wants the creme caramel!' a teenage boy calls out.

He has dreadlocks and braces on his teeth. I like his flannel shirt and his punk attitude, so I give him a smile before I move on to taking coffee orders.

Four lattes, two long blacks, three dessert wines. I write it all down on my notepad, collect up the dessert menus and head for the kitchen.

'Six creme caramels, Davey!' I tear off the page from my notepad and slide it next to the other dessert orders above the stainless-steel bench where Dave plates up.

'Gee, that's a group of original human beings,' he says sarcastically. 'Michael, can you plate up those desserts, mate.'

Michael nods.

'How's that Pines table going, Joni?' Dave asks in a cheeky voice.

'I think they'll be another half hour at least. Has Juliet brought their dessert orders in yet?'

'I just sent her away with their desserts,' says Michael.

'Oh.' I start getting nervous about re-telling my disastrous night to Dave.

Half an hour passes by quickly, and by what feels like ten-thirty, Harland is beginning to empty out. The group who were in the Red Room leave, and I take the last of their dirty cutlery and crockery in to Simon in the kitchen. He hardly talks, mainly grunts.

"Anks,' he half-says.

His baggy skater pants drag in the dirty water on the floor. His hands are beyond prune-like, and his BO is pungent. He seems a sweet guy, though. I mean, he hasn't done anything to upset me, and he doesn't really talk to me, so I pretty much ignore him. I've never really looked long enough into his eyes to know what colour they are. I imagine he skates with his stoner friends, and would possibly refer to me as a snob. But I don't care.

Lucy sits cross-legged at the staff table sipping coffee and flipping through the bookings diary with a dramatic forcefulness. I hear Juliet opening the back door, and bursting into the room announcing, 'The Pines has officially been cleared! Can I knock off now, Lucy Lou? Pleeeease?' She throws her dirty apron in the laundry bag that hangs from the back of the kitchen door.

'Have you cleared Lillibon? Swept the floor?' Lucy snaps.

'Yessiree!' chirps Juliet, saluting like a sailor.

'Okay then, you can knock off,' says Lucy. 'Can you make sure you sign your hours in properly.'

She slides the hours book across the staff table so forcefully that it falls violently at Juliet's feet. Juliet picks it up, not at all bothered by the inappropriate delivery, and scribbles in her hours.

Juliet then announces loudly, 'Drinky poos,' as she helps herself to a wine glass. Bending over to open the low door to the wine fridge, she exhales, 'Awwwwwwww.' It sounds like she's giving birth.

'This is the best stretch.' She straightens her legs and her back, as though someone is about to mount her from behind. I look away, scrunching up my forehead. Dave catches my eye and we both smile, laughing hysterically on the inside.

I glance up at the clock hanging on the wall in the hallway and notice it's almost a quarter to eleven. Harland feels, and sounds, empty, except for a couple in Gatsby who arrived at nine-thirty. Trust my designated area to have the latecomers who hang around forever. I walk in there, hovering, looking for things to clear, trying to make it obvious that my knock-off drink cannot commence until they leave.

I check them out carefully. They're an older couple, probably in their forties or fifties. God, I can't imagine what life would be like at that age. The woman is tipsy, and her cheeks are flushed. Her fluffy green cardigan is open, and her cream blouse is buttoned right to the top. An oval ceramic brooch is pinned where the edges of her collar meet. She has lipstick on her front teeth, but it would be too embarrassing for me to tell her.

'We've seen you coming in and out of the side gate at Peter and Rebecca's,' she says, in a drunken, posh slur.

'Oh,' I say. 'I've been living there for almost six months now.'

'In the little bungalow in the backyard?' the woman asks.

'Yeah.'

'It's such an incredible little place,' she gushes. 'I mean, how gorgeous! Living in a small wooden cabin in the backyard, beside a large gum tree. It's so romantic! If we were young we would have moved in there, sweetie, wouldn't we,' she says flirtatiously to her partner. 'I'm Barb, by the way, and this is John,' she continues.

'Oh, I'm Joni. Joni Johnson.'

We shake hands, which feels weird.

'Peter's a darling,' Barb says, 'and Rebecca is divine. They look so in love.'

She goes on about them for a while, until I interrupt with, 'I only really know Rebecca. We all keep to ourselves a bit. Peter . . . I don't know at all. He's a bit of a mysterious guy.'

'Well, he's always so lost in his work, isn't he,' she says, as though she admires him deeply.

'You know him well?' I ask.

'All playwrights are lost souls, honey,' Barb says in a very confident manner.

She rubs John's arm, as though she's intentionally trying to make him jealous by glorifying Peter's job as a playwright. It's so obvious, otherwise why would she be comforting John with her patronising mid-arm rub.

John doesn't seem to pick up on any of this. 'Well,' he says brightly, 'the meal was incredible tonight!'

It's at this point that I notice Lucy behind me, and of course she takes all the credit.

'Thank you,' she says, acting as though she's backstage after performing the main part in one of Peter's plays, greeting her friends as they throw endless flattering comments towards her.

'We live on the same street as this darling,' Barb tells Lucy.

'Oh! Well, we all love Joni,' says Lucy.

I know she only half-means it.

'We'll grab the bill then, thanks,' says John, cutting short the only kind thing Lucy's said to me tonight.

'Yes, darlings, the bill would be great,' says Barb. 'We should get out of your hair and let you clean up.'

'Joni will organise that for you,' Lucy says, making sure she demonstrates clearly that she's the boss.

I walk out of Gatsby thinking about Peter. He's such a handsome man. But he barely talks to me when I see him up on his back verandah. He's very quiet. Lost in his own world. I guess he's busy inventing characters, working on plots and subplots, composing monologues.

I find the page with Barb and John's order in my notebook, tear it out, fold it, and put it on a floral Royal Albert saucer. I reach into the glass jar on the sideboard for two after-dinner mints, and place them on the saucer with the bill.

'Here we are,' I say, handing it to Barb and John, intentionally keeping the conversation to a minimum. Finally, they walk out together, arm-in-arm.

'You know what time it is?' Lucy says, as I enter the Bar Room.

'Time for knock-off drinks,' I say, smiling.

'And . . .' she says excitedly, leaving me guessing.

4

Turning her back on me, Lucy opens the doors to the sideboard in the hallway. The boys in the kitchen have turned up the radio and 'Doll Parts' by Hole is blasting through to the Bar Room. I'm now well and truly ready to sit down and rest my legs, so I leave Lucy to her business and head straight for the bar.

I reach for a wine glass from the shelf above the bench. There are three styles to choose from. One is a mid-sized crystal glass, the second is a large, more contemporary style of wine glass, and the third (the one I choose) is a wide-brimmed champagne glass with tiny stars etched around the sides. Lucy told me on my first night working at Harland that these champagne glasses were called 'coupes', and that the first ones ever made were modelled on the shape of Marie Antoinette's breast. I remember she spoke loudly, touching her own right breast suggestively, in the hope that all the men in the room witnessed her sensual anecdote.

As I'm placing the champagne coupe on the bench, Tiger-Lily jumps up and rubs against my arm. 'Puss, puss,' I say to her gently, patting her soft fur with my palms which, after everything I've done this evening, are almost back to their regular colour.

I admire the organic nature of Tiger-Lily's coat. The swirling patterns, the stripes, the patches of black and golden beige. So beautiful. I think about the painting I'm working on, the colours I was playing around with today. Am I too obsessed with warm colours? Does the shadow of the figure on the left-hand side of my current painting need to be darker?

Dave calls to me from the kitchen. 'Joni, can you give me a hand with a few boxes in the Pines.'

'Sure.'

I suddenly feel sixteen butterflies take flight inside my tummy, and I swallow nervously while pouring white wine into my glass. I bring the full coupe with me as I follow Dave through the back door and down the stairs towards the Pines. It's freezing, but I notice halfway down that I'm not afraid of the Harland ghost when Dave is by my side.

I'm pathetic. I like to think I'm independent, and a feminist, yet I'm terrified of being alone in the dark on the garden path.

Dave swings open the door to the Pines, pulls a chair out from the table, and takes a seat.

'Okay, tell me all about last night, Joni.'

I feel as if I'm about to be psychoanalysed, as if Dave is my therapist, even though I've never had therapy before. However, when he slouches and places his sweaty hands on his dirty apron, flicking aside the stray hairs that dangle in front of his face, my Freudian fantasy dissipates.

I sit anxiously in the chair beside him, placing my right elbow on the table, resting my head in my hand. 'I lost my virginity last night.'

'Jesus, Joni! I didn't know you were a virgin! How old are you?'

'Twenty-one.'

'Christ, you're twenty-one and still a virgin?'

I slowly run my fingers over the knife and fork lying either side of the serviette in front of me, and begin to regret having confided in Dave.

'Who was it? Who was the lucky boy?'

He's poking fun at me now.

'That guy Brendan.'

'What guy Brendan? What's his surname?'

'I don't know his last name!' I yell back at Dave. 'He's the guy who works behind the bar at the Emerald. The blond guy with the clean-cut hair, who always wears beige pants and a polo shirt. The one we pay out all the time.'

'Oh! Joni, Joni,' Dave cries in disbelief.

'I know. What am I doing, Dave? What—am—I—doing?'

'Losing my virginity,' Dave sings to the tune of 'Losing My Religion', doing his best Michael Stipe impersonation. 'You're looking for love in all the wrong places, Joni.'

I sigh and think back to early this morning, in Brendan's room in his Rozelle share house. I was naked, on his bed. He was beside me, stroking my arm, trying to make eye contact with me, but I was looking away. He'd then slowly climbed on top of me and kissed me on the lips. His kisses were beautiful, soft, wet kisses, but I could not feel the spark. I could not connect with his mind. The most passionate thing he said to me was, 'Move over.'

He is undeniably handsome, in a *Beverly Hills, 90210* sort of way. His chiselled jaw, his full lips, the little dimple on his left cheek when he smiles. I won't deny that my fifteen-year-old self would have been attracted to him. But further education, plus art school, plus general day-to-day development in acquiring taste, means it's easy for me to see that Brendan is not my type. It needed to happen though—I needed to not be a virgin anymore.

Dave and I had made fun of Brendan when we'd once ended up at the Emerald for another round of drinks after work. His cocky confidence and the slow way he collected all the dirty schooner glasses, stacking them in a tower and leaning them against his buffed-up body. The way he attempted to flirt with every girl who ordered a drink from him. And the sleazy way he'd rub his fingers on your palm when he gave you your change. Brendan really is quite repulsive, but now that I've seen his wiener and we've actually had sex, I feel sorry for him. All that shit we'd given him. But God, I can't deny that I am relieved to have lost my virginity.

Did it hurt? Yes. In more ways than one. Physically; and, after witnessing Dave's horrified reaction, I can see that sleeping with Brendan has damaged my social reputation. But at least I know that I won't die a virgin, which has been one of my greatest fears.

I even used to imagine the headstone on my grave: *Joni Johnson. Virgin.* Although, if I die tonight, the engraving on my headstone could be even worse: *Joni Johnson. Died tragically, soon after losing her virginity to Brendan 'Beige Pants' (surname unknown).*

'You're a late bloomer, Joni,' Dave says to me slowly, emphasising *late*. 'The latest bloomer I know.' Great. 'And he is not your type.'

'I am aware of that,' I snap.

'I've got to give you some love advice, girl,' Dave says. 'How did you go through art school without having sex with anyone?'

'I don't know, I just did. I almost got together with someone, but he ended up going out with Annabelle.'

'There you go, that's why. Annabelle stole all your potential lovers.'

'That's not true! Leave her alone! You know she's my best friend and I love her to bits.'

He is partially right, actually, but I'm missing Annabelle too much to admit it. She's been away in London almost three months now, and I've only spoken to her on the phone once. Mainly because she's been so busy, but international calls are so expensive, I get worried that if I call her again, my phone bill will tip me over the edge and I'll be broke for weeks.

'I need to get back to the kitchen and clean up,' Dave says, rising from his chair. 'We'll talk more later, Joni—or is that Virgin Mother Mary?'

'Shut up.' I try to hold back a smile as he hilariously performs the Catholic Father-Son-and-Holy-Spirit hand gesture on his way out.

I follow him, my mind filled with embarrassment and shame over my poor selection of playmate. I even gave Brendan my phone number. What was I thinking? God help me if he calls me! Dave runs ahead of me, and bounces up the back stairs. Instead of going back inside, I choose to give myself some time out in the outhouse toilet.

It's beyond freezing in there, and when I pull my dress up and slide my tights down, my legs and bum turn to ice as soon as they make contact with the wooden toilet seat. I think back to this morning when I was at Brendan's, how he took my art journal out of my bag.

He found my notes on David Hockney's *Mr and Mrs Clark and Percy*. 'He painted it in 1981,' he said to me.

'No, it was the early seventies, actually,' I called back to him, applying some black eyeliner while looking in the tiny mirror I keep in the front pocket of my backpack.

'The cat sitting on the man's lap is supposed to be some type of symbol, but I think it's just a cat, for god's sake. It's a cat looking out the window. Probably a hungry cat. A cat who wants his food. Meow! Feed me, Mummy,' he said in a comedic voice that, to be honest, was funny. But it left me feeling downhearted. I gave him a little laugh. How could he not appreciate or understand symbolism in art?

'We studied David Hockney last year,' I said. 'The cat is a symbol of infidelity and envy.'

'Whatever,' he threw back, uninterested.

'It's a painting that reminds me of my friend Annabelle, ' I said, though I regretted opening up to Brendan as soon as the words left my mouth. 'I'm envious of her, and she had a thing with a married man last year.'

'Who is this Annabelle? I want to meet her,' he said in a disgustingly flirty manner. Like all men, he seemed more interested in her than in me.

By this stage all I wanted was to get out of his house, but he continued flipping through the pages of my art journal. 'Mmmm.' He quoted, *'Just as the pious man prays without speaking a word and the Almighty harkens unto him, so the artist with true feelings paints and the sensitive man understands and recognises it.'*

'That's Caspar David Friedrich.'

'From the Romantic movement,' read Brendan. 'I always hated studying poems from the Romantic period in English. Hated it! The language. So flowery and over the top.'

I began to realise that the more Brendan said, the more I felt that he was my polar opposite. We had nothing in common except for being human and living in Sydney. I remember I kept my eyes open during our goodbye kiss in the hallway of his house, staring at the crack in the wall. Then I walked outside, jumped on my bike, and rode home as fast as my legs could take me.

The whole ride home I was thinking how I needed a little darkness in a man, some confusion, or a quick wit. I needed an artist, a poet, a philosopher, a filmmaker. Not clean, boring, simple-minded Brendan, who had no appreciation for the arts. Someone who was a deep thinker, who would talk things over with me. Someone like Michael Nyman, when he was in the midst of composing the score for *The Piano*. Someone with that impassioned, creative intensity.

Sitting on the now warmed-up seat in the outhouse toilet at Harland, I let my imagination take my Michael Nyman fantasy to a whole new level. I imagine Michael Nyman and me living in an apartment in Paris. I'd have my own little studio, and he'd work in the lounge room with the window open. Long white curtains would billow inwards, and then fly back out again, lightly touching the red geraniums in ceramic pots on the sunlit balcony. Michael would spend the day composing on a luxurious black grand piano. His music would drift into my studio, inspiring me throughout the day, while I'd be producing my best work to date. Then he'd come to me in the early evening. I'd be in some gorgeous cream silk, floor-length nightie that he would have bought me on one of our romantic strolls along the Champs-Élysées. The Paradise for Dead Heroes—I've always loved that. He'd grab hold of me around my waist with his large, strong hands, and then, like a published poet, he'd passionately confess that I was what made him complete. His words would sound something like the lyrics to a second verse of a Leonard Cohen song, but Michael would have thought them up himself, on the spur of the moment. He'd look me in the eyes, deeply connecting with my soul, and he'd explain to me that I was what inspired these love poems, that I was what drove him to compose his emotional, heartbreaking music.

Ah, Joni, get over yourself. It's never going to happen. I pull the chain and feel ridiculously immature for letting myself get so carried away with my mid-wee Michael Nyman fantasy.

I realise I've been in the outhouse toilet for an unusually long time. People will be thinking I can't flush my giant poo, or I've got diarrhoea, or worse, that I'm uncomfortably constipated. Straightening my dress, taking in a deep breath, I exit and climb the stairs back up into Harland. The warmth and chattering of my co-workers takes my mind off how much I hate myself for being such a daydreaming, late-blooming loser.

The first thing that grabs my attention is Lucy who, I notice, is leaning over what looks like an old record player. 'Kill that radio in the kitchen, would you, Davey,' she orders loudly.

'Party pooper!' yells Dave, peeking around the doorway. Then he quickly changes his tune: 'Oh, gramophone time! Old-fashioned dance hall time!'

'I thought you were saving this up for the winter staff dinner!' Juliet calls out to Lucy, untwisting the wire on the top of a champagne bottle. The cork pops, rebounding from the ceiling straight into my shoulder.

'Ouch,' I shriek. 'Juliet!'

'Joni, let me fill your glass, sweetheart.'

Lucy closes the restaurant and holds two staff dinners each year. A summertime one—which I went to in January, and loved—and a winter dinner, which is coming up in about six weeks. Two of her schoolfriends from France joined us for the summertime dinner, and Lucy brought out a box of dress-ups, and we all carried on dancing and drinking until the wee hours of the morning. It was incredibly fun. Crazy fun, actually. I'm so excited for the upcoming winter one.

I scull my remaining wine and hand Juliet my coupe. She fills it to the brim. Lucy meanwhile dumps a pile of incredibly old records on the table. I can see some of the sleeves look off-white, tea-stained. I head straight for the pile. I love music, although I've never learnt an instrument. Taking a sip of bubbly champagne, I lick my lips and start sifting through the pile of records. I find a cover I like.

'"A Fine Romance" by Fred Astaire,' I share with the room. 'From the film *Swing Time*.'

'Never heard of it.' Michael has suddenly come to life after his first beer.

Dave and Simon join us in the Bar Room, both throwing their aprons in the dirty laundry basket.

'Bubbles?' asks Juliet.

'Sure, I'll have a glass,' Dave says with enthusiasm.

'I'm going straight for a beer,' Simon says, reaching into the fridge.

'So, ladies and gentlemen, these records and this wind-up

gramophone were purchased by *moi* at a garage sale last weekend. All the records are from the thirties, and I'm going to start the night with . . .' Lucy reads out the label on the record she's placed on the gramophone, '"Begin the Beguine".' She squints a little. 'By Artie Shaw and His Orchestra.'

Lucy winds up the gramophone, her gold bracelets moving back and forth elegantly on her slender wrist. 'Begin the Beguine' starts up, and it's such a cute little song I can't help calling out, 'Oh my god, this is so *Annie Hall!*'

'Woody Allen?' asks Juliet.

'Yeah. It's like the music he has in his films,' I say, taking another sip of champagne.

'I love the clarinet solo,' says Dave, showing off to everyone that he can actually tell what instrument is playing. He's like Annabelle—really musical.

Lucy downs a shot of port from an ornate crystal glass, slamming it on the bench when she's done. She begins to dance, mimicking the moves of a sassy whore in an Italian arthouse film. I don't know anyone else who drinks port except Annabelle's grandparents. Lucy, of course, somehow manages to make everyone around her want to drink whatever she's drinking.

'Watcha!' Dave invents some weird word and joins in with a mix of karate moves followed by overly enthusiastic *West Side Story* finger snaps. The music sounds so quaint and old-fashioned, it's adorable. I smile widely and swing my hips in time, closing my eyes for a moment. Juliet joins in next, with a bottle of champagne in her hand, topping up glasses. She pokes her boobs out, lifting her right shoulder and then her left—up and down, up and down to the beat. The sight of her dancing makes me want to puke. She's so uncool, it hurts.

Placing the bottle on the bench, she transitions from Boobs-Out Dance to Crazy Exotic Indian Hand Movement Dance. Neither style resembles the dancing style of the 1930s at all. Not that I really know what the 1930s dancing style is.

A friend of Simon's rocks up through the back door and sits with him at the table. There's no chance in hell they'll get up and dance. Simon lights up a joint, and the whole room starts to smell like pot. Tiger-Lily arches her back elegantly as she walks across the table through the smoky fog.

I love my life, I think, followed closely by *I feel a bit tipsy.*

I check out more of the records in the pile while Dave, Juliet and Lucy continue dancing.

'Oh my god!' I cry out. 'Here's a song called "That Cat Is High"—and check out Tiger-Lily! She's breathing in all your stinky pot smoke, Simon!'

Everybody laughs.

'Put it on! Put it on!' shouts Dave, spilling his champagne mid-spin.

Fumbling with the gramophone, I carefully place the record on the turntable and bring the arm across.

'So funny,' says Dave, making me feel really good.

Lucy pours herself another full glass of port and holds it in her hand while she starts sexy dancing with her back against Juliet. I put the Fred Astaire record back in the sleeve, and place it gently on top of the pile. Shimmying backwards, I gradually move in closer to the dancefloor action. I turn to face the others, and literally two seconds later Lucy starts pashing Juliet.

Eeww, this is awkward and weird. An up-close-and-personal view of my boss giving a sloppy tongue kiss to Juliet.

'Woooooo!' cries Dave, holding his hands up in the air.

So she's bisexual too. Lucy Bourdillon, sexpot extraordinaire!

'That Cat Is High' gets flipped off pretty quickly, and someone puts on a slower number. Dave and I embrace, and do some silly, over-the-top ballroom dancing moves. Lucy lights up a cigarette and blows out a full puff of smoke.

Juliet goes in for another kiss, but Lucy pushes her away. 'Don't!' she says sharply, demonstrating that she purely made the move on Juliet to shock me and Dave.

Even after her rejection by Lucy, Juliet displays a new-found confidence. She closes her eyes, reaching her arms out wide for more of her ugly Indian finger dancing. I can tell what she's thinking, and it's in a bragging tone, on repeat: *Lucy just kissed me, Lucy just kissed me, Lucy just kissed me.*

5

'I should get going,' I announce to the group.

Michael is sitting with Simon and Simon's mate Chris. They've been talking politics all night. Well, Michael's been talking politics all night; right now he's preaching to Simon and Chris about the dangers of John Howard possibly being elected prime minister. Simon and Chris look stoned and uninterested, just nodding, only half-listening.

Poor Michael. He's like a sad dad with a kind heart. He always seems a little melancholic and despondent, except for when it comes to discussing politics—particularly his faith in the Greens, and his dislike of right-wing policies. His face lights up and his eyebrows rise and fall with his in-depth descriptions of party members and former leaders he approves of. But I do feel for him a bit. He doesn't really fit in with me, Dave, Lucy and Juliet, and he is also unlike Simon.

'See ya Joni!' he calls out.

'Bye! See you tomorrow night.'

Juliet offers me another glass of champagne, even though

she clearly heard that I'm planning to leave. I decline, feeling irritated. She's desperate to keep the party going, but we're all saying no to another round. Instead, Lucy reminds everyone that it's Friday night, suggesting to Dave and Juliet that they move on to the Emerald for a few more drinks.

'Wonder who's working behind the bar tonight?' Dave winks at me, making it much too obvious.

'Why do you want to know who's working behind the bar?' Lucy asks.

Dave and I act busy, hoping that Lucy will leave it alone, which she does, thank god.

I grab my beret and slide it onto my head, tucking my hair up underneath it. I notice Dave gazing at me, up and down, for an unusually long time, and I feel slightly uncomfortable.

'I'll come with you, Joni,' he says. 'I rode in tonight too.'

I'm surprised that Dave decides to leave at the same time as me. He nearly always stays back later. He grabs his backpack from the base of the hatstand and plonks it on the table beside me as I put on my black cardigan, followed by my jacket. Lucy looks over at Dave and me, unafraid of exposing her envious scowl. It's so obvious she wishes Dave had chosen to go to the Emerald with her, as opposed to riding home with me.

'I'll come with you, Lucy,' Juliet offers.

'I don't want to go now. I'm tired.'

Lucy reaches for her large brown handbag, and dramatically dumps it on the table. She packs up the wind-up gramophone and carries it back into the hallway, looking grumpy and pissed off. The sound of her fumbling around opening and closing cupboard doors drowns out my 'Thanks for bringing out the gramophone tonight, Lucy!' I add, 'See you all tomorrow,' as I head towards the back door.

'Hang on, Joni,' Dave says. 'I've just got to close up in here, and I wanna get changed.'

I wait patiently. He's taking forever.

'Davey!' I howl in a tired voice towards the kitchen.

'Yep, coming.'

The lights in the kitchen finally flick off, and Dave walks towards me. He's changed out of his greasy chequered chef pants and stained white top, and is now wearing blue jeans, black Converse boots and a red-checked flannel shirt. He has a beaten-up denim jacket in his hand and he's pushing one arm through the sleeve, trying to get it on as quickly as possible.

'Let's go, girl.'

I feel kind of special when he says that. I suddenly have a warm feeling between my legs, and wonder whether I might be attracted to Dave. This feels weird. Maybe I'm just tipsy. I look at his face. Yep, just tipsy. Nothing there.

We walk out into the freezing cold and attempt to disentangle our bikes from each other. They've been resting together side by side against the wall of the shed all night. Dave suggests that our bikes are romantically involved. We giggle as our frozen fingers untangle the handlebars, and I scream, 'It's fucking freezing!'

Once we're out the front of Harland, we put our helmets on. I drop my bag into my basket and Dave takes off ahead of me. I look towards the moonlit harbour; its beauty is overwhelming. The night is so crisp I can hardly feel my face, but I still manage to smile. My boots push on the pedals, and the wheels of my bike turn. The chain makes its rhythmic squeak, and I finally catch up to Dave.

We pass the rows of small cottages with bare winter gardens. There's not a cloud in the sky, just stars, and an almost full moon. My warm breath makes a beautiful fog in front of me. It's times like this when I feel most alive. I feel free, and at one with the world and everything around me. We once talked about nature during drawing class, and about the twelve signs of the zodiac being divided into four elements: fire, earth, air, water. I certainly do not believe in star signs, but it's moments like these—riding home in the middle of a freezing cold winter's night—that I do believe in. It's an invigorating version of euphoria. But I don't want to arrive home to no one; I want someone to come home to.

We ride past the Emerald, and I keep my head down, focusing on the road, hoping desperately that Brendan doesn't see me. An awful ache in the depths of my stomach reconfirms how much I regret having slept with him last night. I look ahead to where Dave has stopped on the side of the road—this is where I turn off and he'll continue on.

I roll up beside him. 'See ya mate,' he says.

'Thanks for hearing me out tonight.'

'No worries. See you tomorrow.'

He takes off, and I watch him get smaller and smaller, further and further away from me. The strands of my hair that managed to escape being tucked under my beret and helmet flick across my face as I make a right-hand turn towards my place. Almost home. It's around about now that I start thinking about my pillow, and my bed, and the feeling of hot water from the shower running over my body. Cup of tea, piece of toast. Mmmm, I can't wait.

The streetlight on the corner of my street shines down on the large gum tree I can see from my bungalow. The web of shadows created by the branches makes an abstract pattern on the road. I think about my painting again. About the shapes I'm filling in, in the lower section of the canvas. And then that's interrupted by the thought of Dave. His face, when I felt all warm and fuzzy, just before we left Harland. Maybe he'd be an okay option for me? Maybe I could have a go at being his girlfriend? I think he might like me? Nah, he's just a friend. But we get on.

Now that I'm an expert with boys, I should be able to work this out in my head. Maybe we could just be sex buddies? No, that's so not me. That's Annabelle's style. It needs to be all or nothing for me. And last night—ugh. It was worse than nothing. I won't let anything ever, ever develop with Brendan. I'd rather cut my hands off and never be able to paint again than pursue a relationship with him.

I pull up beside my gate, which is tricky to open. I have to reach my arm up high and over, unhooking the latch on the other side. I wheel my bike through, over the grass that's covered with fallen gum leaves, bark and twigs. I look towards my backyard bungalow, its front door facing the gate. Someone's on my doorstep.

Oh my god—it's Annabelle!

6

Sitting in the dark, she glows. Her hair looks a little different, but it's still bleached blonde, in a messy bob. Her adorably chubby legs are covered with cream ribbed woollen tights, and her arms are wrapped around them in an attempt to keep warm. Her velvety faux fur black coat—its collar curled up around her neck—makes her porcelain face look angelic. Below her coat, her denim skirt is so short it's barely visible. Once she notices me, she spreads her arms wide and calls out, 'Joni!'

I drop my bike on the grass and run to her, giving her the warmest embrace possible. 'Shhh!' I say, concerned that she'll wake the neighbours. I continue, in an excited loud whisper. 'What are you doing here? My god, it's so good to see you!'

Tears well up in my eyes, and Annabelle pulls back from the hug and looks at me lovingly.

'Stop it,' she says. 'Now you've got me going.' She begins to cry, and we hug each other tighter.

'I have so much to tell you,' she blubbers, sniffing loudly, and pulling away from me. She wipes her tears from her cheeks. 'I just flew in from New York.'

'What?'

'Well, via LA. I arrived this morning. I've been at Mum's sleeping, but I desperately needed to see you.'

'I thought you were in London?'

'I was, but I ended up in New York. I have so much to tell you, Joni,' she repeats.

'Come in, it's so cold out here.'

I walk back to get my bike, and wheel it up onto the verandah of my bungalow. I fumble around for my keys in my bag, and quickly unlock the front door.

'Ah, smells like Joni,' Annabelle says, taking in a deep breath.

Once we're both inside Annabelle flops on my comfy light brown couch. My keys jingle as I toss them towards the wooden kitchen bench, then a deadened metallic clap follows as they land. I light the gas heater and, once the blue flame turns the grate orange, lift my finger off the switch.

'Mind if I put a record on?' Annabelle asks.

'Go for it,' I tell her, and suddenly it feels like she has never been away, we've never been apart.

She chooses *Dummy* by Portishead, but the slow groove of the first song is quickly drowned out by our conversation.

'What were you doing in New York? Why are you back so early? Weren't you supposed to be coming home in September?'

I walk into the kitchen, fill the kettle, and turn it on. Annabelle follows me closely, ignoring all my questions.

'Joni.' She holds onto both my arms and looks me in the eyes. 'I'm in love. *I'm in love*, I'M IN LOVE,' she says, with a great crescendo. She lets go of my arms, swishes her hair out of her face and sits up on the bench. Then—*BANG!*—she bumps her head on the cupboard.

'Ouch!'

I smile brightly, and we both burst out laughing. I've missed her so much. Her sparky blue eyes, and her exhilarating spirit. Her presence gives me a new surge of energy, and I've completely forgotten how tired I was when I finished up at Harland.

She reaches for the open bottle of red wine sitting on my bench. I hand her a glass, and make myself a cup of tea.

My bungalow is open-plan, except for the bathroom. The couch is pretty much in the middle of the room, and I have a corner studio space set up diagonally opposite the small kitchen. My bed is on a mezzanine level, and was the deciding point for renting the place. The ladder stairs that lead up to my bed are a light-coloured grainy wood, and the ceiling is lined with darker timber panels.

I sit down slowly on the right-hand cushion of my couch, curling my legs up under the multicoloured crocheted rug while balancing my full cup of tea. Annabelle sits in the left corner of the couch, wine in hand.

'So what's his name?'

'Johnny. Johnny Harrison. You know him? Have you heard of him?'

'No.'

'Okay, so I was in London, touring and stuff. The shows went well, by the way. Really well, actually. Like, people lined up down the street for some of them, waiting to get in, get their spot up in the front row. It was crazy, Joni. I don't want to sound like I'm up myself or anything, but I'm really popular over there. It's insane.'

'It's what you've always wanted,' I tell her kindly.

'I know, but I can't believe it's actually happening. What I dreamed of is becoming a reality.'

'I knew you'd be massive. You're such a great songwriter, Annabelle. And your shows . . .' I take a sip of tea, 'your shows are incredible.'

I mean what I say, but subconsciously I lower my eyes and stare into my teacup. I've always felt second-best compared to Annabelle. Second-best, with barely any talent.

'So Johnny . . . oh wait, wait,' Annabelle says, taking a quick sip from her wine glass. 'Before I got together with Johnny . . . well . . . yeah, this is pretty funny. We'd played about five shows, and then I had a massive fight with Paul. You know, my new bass player. Did you meet him?'

'Yep, the incredibly good-looking guy who used to play with—'

'Yeah, yeah,' she interrupts. 'So Pauly and I have this massive fight. He was being such a prick. And then he threatened to leave my band. We were in Norwich, having a pub dinner—fish and chips—before the show. Then Paul, in a complete turnaround, made this crazy declaration in front of all of us, saying he was in love with me, and . . . Aw, it was so embarrassing. Everyone in the pub could hear him. I mean, you know, I'm flattered and everything, but god, Joni, he's not my type. I had to reject him in front of everyone. Whole pub listening in.'

Annabelle stops talking and stands, puts her wine glass on the kitchen table, and takes her coat off. I remain seated, feeling like her fourteen-year-old sister—in awe of her, jealous, and way behind everything she's experiencing. I swear, every boy she comes in contact with falls for her. At least, that's what it seems like from where I sit. But I'm also envious of her superstar lifestyle. She's pretty famous here in Australia. Her debut album was in the charts, she's been on the cover of music magazines, the subject of full-length articles in the major papers. Before she left for the UK, she was playing big venues here—in Sydney, Melbourne, all around the country. And now she's working with a manager who's trying to break her into the UK.

I watch her as she drinks the remainder of her wine. I'm aware of the fact that my facial expression may be revealing my inner thoughts, so I attempt to perk up and look as though I know how annoying it is to have men falling at my feet.

'So then,' she continues, 'I end up in New York.'

'How did . . . Man, I've always wanted to go back to New York. I haven't been there since—'

She cuts in. 'My UK label thought it would be a good idea for me to do a duet with someone. Boost my profile. So they sent me to New York, because they found out that Johnny Harrison is in love with my music.'

'Who's Johnny . . .'

'He's pretty much the coolest thing in indie music at the moment. I don't think anyone in Australia knows about him yet. I mean, some people do.'

'Wow, okay, so . . .'

'So I arrive in New York, go straight to Johnny Harrison's loft apartment in Brooklyn, and we start writing together. He plays guitar. Incredible musician and songwriter.' Annabelle looks over towards the kitchen. 'Do you mind if I have another wine?'

'Oh yeah, sure, sure.'

She helps herself as I begin to feel more and more incompetent.

'So I get to Johnny's and, fuck, Joni, he's twenty times more good-looking in real life. Like the sexiest guy you've ever seen.

So anyway, blah blah blah, we write a song together, go out to dinner. To cut a long story short, we end up in bed and, yeah, now we're madly in love with each other, and he's coming to Sydney! Hopefully in about four weeks.'

'Wow,' I say, deflating.

'Because . . .' She tops her wine glass right up. 'Because he's moving here!'

'What?'

'Yep. Moving here to be with me. He's choosing ME over New York. Can you believe it? I'm so in love with him, Joni. So unbelievably in love!' Annabelle sits back on the couch, radiating. 'So what about you?' she asks, and my confidence dips to an all-time low.

'Um . . . I've been working on paintings for my group show. The one I've got coming up later in the year.' I squirm a little on the couch and my cheeks heat up. 'And . . . Harland. I've been working at Harland.'

'Oh, I love that place . . . And Daniel? Is that his name?'

'Dave. Yeah, Dave and I have become really good friends.' I bite my nails for a bit. 'So . . . yeah, that's about it.'

Annabelle, with attitude and spark, ruffles up her short hair with her right hand.

'A-and . . .' I add, drawing out the vowel.

'And what? This sounds interesting.'

'I'm really embarrassed to tell you this, but . . . um, I know it's about time . . . I lost my virginity last night.'

'Whaaaat! Joni, that's massive!!! Okay, who was it, who was it?' She bounces on the couch, and leans in towards me.

'Agh, Brendan. This guy from the Emerald.' My chest collapses.

'Your local? That pub?'

'Yeah. So . . .' I explain, 'he's a fucking dork. You'd hate him.'

'Really?' she asks.

'Really.'

'Well,' she says, licking her lips, 'it's good that it's out of the way, anyway.'

'Exactly,' I tell her, glad that she's on my wavelength. 'Worst thing to come out of it is that I gave him my number.'

'Don't worry. He won't call.'

I feel terrible after she says this. He won't call—because I'm hopeless in bed? I'm ugly? A total loser? Is that what she's trying to say? I walk over and put my empty teacup on the kitchen bench.

Annabelle follows. 'Do you think it might be okay for me to stay here for a few weeks? Until I find somewhere to rent?'

'Oh my god, of course,' I tell her. It'll be fun having her stay, even though I feel like a bit of a failure around her. 'But I'm super tired right now. Do you mind if I . . .'

'Me too,' she says, sounding wide awake.

'You okay with the couch? You've slept on it before, it's really . . .'

'Yeah, the couch is great. Thanks, Joni, thank you so much.'

I yawn a big, slow, mouth-wide-open yawn. 'You'll have to tell me more about your tour in the morning.'

'Yeah . . . Man, so much to tell you.'

We hug, and I wash my makeup off in the bathroom. I climb the ladder stairs to my bed and get changed into my jammies.

'Night!' I call out to Annabelle from up high.

'Night!' she calls out from the bathroom, her mouth full of toothbrush and toothpaste.

7

Almost a month later, Annabelle is still sleeping on my couch. It's been so nice re-connecting, hearing further details about her tour—the ups and, of course, the emotional downs. There were lots of those, apparently. And I'm still managing to get heaps of painting done, 'cause she's been rehearsing with her band four days a week. I love having her here, although I suspect I might start to tire of it soon. But at least she's giving me money towards the rent, and she's putting in for food. And she never uses my phone to call Johnny Harrison. She goes up the street to the pay phone for that.

She's been to check out a few share houses. But both places housed students who were huge fans of her music. She told me it would have been a total nightmare if she'd moved in with those 'kids'.

I keep telling her she needs to find her own place. No housemates. Like me. She claims she's so busy with rehearsals and meetings, she hardly has the time to apply for a rental. Even though she's famous, she doesn't have that much money, so her living with me is a pretty good deal financially. Maybe she's dragging out her time staying here because she secretly wants to wait until Johnny arrives, then they can go house hunting together. Who knows.

Harland's been kinda busy. Busier than usual, actually. And Dave's been . . . overly nice to me. Or just a bit different. Maybe it's just my imagination. I have to admit that, since my Brendan episode, I've realised how beautiful it would be to have intimate, physical contact with someone on a regular basis. Besides, I always imagined I'd have a boyfriend by the time I was twenty-one. I remember thinking that in high school, when most of my friends were already going out with someone.

But I need to find a boy who has the polar opposite personality type to Brendan. Which maybe Dave has? He's kind and . . . interested. He always includes me in the group conversations during knock-off drinks. And he was the first one to ask me all about my life, and my art practice. He's the first one to stand up for me when Lucy has a go at me, which she does most nights.

I love his funny anecdotes about stuff he did when he was younger. Like how he was an extra on *Home and Away*. 'Three episodes!' he half-bragged, half-joked. That was when he thought he wanted to be an actor. When he was on the set of *Home and Away*, he mainly hung out at the catering truck, and talked food with the caterers, but he didn't see the signs and still desperately wanted to become an actor. After two failed auditions for parts in low-budget films, he gave up on the whole actor idea and enrolled in an evening cooking class that took place at the high school near his house. And that's where, he said, he found his calling.

'*You shall be a chef!*' Dave called out loudly, as we all sat around the staff table, listening to his story. His low-toned, theatrical delivery sounded as though he was doing the voice of God. It was hilarious.

And I love the path he took towards becoming a chef. Unlike most Sydney chefs, who simply go to hospitality school here in Australia, Dave chose his favourite cuisine—French—and researched the best cooking school in the South of France—his preferred part of the country. He saved up, applied, got in, and moved over there. He rented a room in a dilapidated farmhouse, and mornings consisted of him sitting with bohemian French folk, drinking coffee in the overgrown garden. During the day he attended the culinary school, and learnt the delicate skills and fundamental rules of cooking the French way. And in true Dave style, along with his French cooking education, he also picked up the language, and delved into the history of the local area. And he did this while consciously hanging tight onto his Aussie accent and his humorous outlook on life.

Anyway, when Dave returned from France and started looking for employment in Sydney, he got thrown in the deep end, working as an assistant chef at a French restaurant in Bondi. A year into his Bondi stint, he looked for work as a head chef, already feeling confident that he was ready for the top position. At the same time, that exact position became available at Harland. Dave took the interview with Lucy, did two trial nights, and got the job.

He has said once or twice that he'd love to own his own restaurant one day, which I know he will, because he's such a positive go-getter. But he never mentions this around Lucy, which I think is out of kindness and his desire to promote *good vibes* (his words, I would never say that) within the walls of Harland.

I don't think he's had a girlfriend for a while. When he told me all about his time at the French cooking school, he said he had been seeing someone. 'She was a lousy lover' was the only info he shared on that particular subject.

I dunno. Dave and me. Would that work? Romantically? Possibly? I wouldn't want things to go weird at work though. I love my job at Harland. And I like my life right now. Painting, waitressing, sleeping. It's divided into thirds, and all three segments are rolling along nicely. And now that Annabelle's back, everything seems ten times more exciting.

We were up pretty late last night, watching telly, talking. I'm really tired, and although I woke up a while ago, I haven't managed to get out of bed yet. I lean over and look down at the large canvas sitting on the easel. A rush of excitement runs through my body, which helps me feel more awake. I'm onto my second painting for the group show, and it brings me a sense of satisfaction seeing how far I've come with it. I want to get a lot more work done today, before I head off to Harland for my shift. A little more sleep would have been good though.

I look over towards the couch. That's weird. Where's Annabelle? Walking down the steep wooden ladder stairs, my legs feel a little wobbly. I grab my big woolly cardigan, then notice a note on the kitchen bench.

Morning Joni,
I'm heading back to Mum's to get some clothes and things. I'll

be back this arvo. I've got the spare key, so I can let myself in if you're already at work. Thanks heaps for letting me stay here. It should only be for a couple more weeks.
Love Annabelle xo

I turn the heater on, warm my hands, then make myself a coffee. The sweet red-and-white chequered curtain in the kitchen covers the side window, which faces Rebecca and Peter's house. I pull it back, and there they are, sitting on their back verandah steps. They're both reading the paper, and the image of them sitting there together looks like a scene composed for a *Vogue Living* photo shoot. I give them a wave. Rebecca gives a friendly wave back, and Peter just smiles.

I drag myself over to the couch, where Annabelle has left the crocheted rug and spare blanket neatly folded. I take a long, savouring sip of my coffee, and glance over at my painting, feeling full to the brim with creative energy.

I wee, and take a long look at myself in the bathroom mirror. My blue eyes—bloodshot. My brown hair—messed up. When I shower, the warm water heats my body. I towel dry, and walk quickly over to my clothes rack, the floorboards cooling the soles of my feet each time they touch down.

Once I'm dressed in my paint-stained navy overalls, with a cream woollen jumper underneath, I make myself some toast. Peanut butter and honey, sliced apple, and another coffee. I put *The Velvet Underground & Nico* on my record player, and the first song, 'Sunday Morning', floats through my bungalow. It's one of my favourite songs. And then I hold a paintbrush in my hand, and squint, and tilt my head this way and that, lining up the wooden brush with the circular shape in the upper right corner of my painting. And then I take a deep breath, and ask myself, *Is this making me feel anything? Anything at all?*

And then I don't even answer myself, because I know it is.

Without hesitation, I continue on where I left off yesterday. The music gives me that extra sense of On-Top-of-the-Worldness. I feel so inspired and, dare I say, ON FIRE! I go with it, working nonstop for a few hours.

In between my time in front of the canvas, I rinse brushes, flip records, consume more coffee, and eventually take a break. I flop on the couch, and stare at the poster of Goethe's colour wheel on my wall. I've always been so intrigued by his theories—how he thought that colours were linked to emotions.

I walk over to one of my art folders, and flip through until I find the image of Goethe's earlier 'Rose of Temperaments'. Then I read over all my notes. *Character traits or personality types are matched to different colours. Heroes, lovers, poets—all paired with different colours.* Freshly inspired, I walk back over to my canvas. It's a portrait of Annabelle and me, inspired by a photograph from that night we first met, at one of her shows. My palette is spotted with imperfect circles of rich reds, mellow ambers and bright yellows, like the feathers of the budgerigar I had when I was a kid. I pick up a brush, and think a little bit about Dave, and how we get on so well.

Then I force myself to get on top of my wandering mind. Okay, my painting. What am I trying to portray? The emotional connection. The energy exchanged between two people. The unspoken language of attraction, whether it be sexual or platonic. I'm still so into this as a theme for my works for the group show.

After two further hours or so of contentedly working away,

the phone rings. Shit, my hands are so dirty, I hate it when this happens. I wipe them quickly on my overalls, run to the kitchen bench and answer the phone.

'Hello?'

'It's me, Annabelle.'

'Hey, how's your day going?'

'Oh my god, amazing! I'm at Mum's place, just getting my stuff together. I called my manager today, and he said the most incredible thing.'

'What?'

'Okay, well, George—from my label in the UK—he played the duet I recorded with Johnny Harrison to one of the writers from *Dazed & Confused* magazine. And guess what?'

'Um, can't guess.'

'She's flying out to Sydney next week! A woman who writes for *Dazed & Confused*! She'll be interviewing me about what it was like to work with Johnny, and how my album is the hidden gem of nineteen ninety-five. How I'm going to be the next big thing in the UK!'

'That's amazing, Annabelle!' I am genuinely excited for her. She deserves this. I knew this day would come.

'Okay, okay. So there's a photographer coming too. Some guy from London. They want to interview me over dinner, and photograph me somewhere interesting. I'm wondering if you think it might be an okay idea for the writer to interview me at Harland? It's two weeks from tomorrow.'

'Sure. That sounds great! I'll just check with Lucy tonight. You should do it in the Red Room!'

'Oh yeah. I love the Red Room. That's a great idea, Joni.'

'When will you be back here?'

'I've got heaps of running around to do, so probably not until eight or so.'

'Okay. There's pasta and sweet potato and broccoli here. Enough to make yourself some dinner.'

There's a moment of silence. 'Thanks, Joni. I gotta go.'

'Okay, bye,' I tell her.

'Bye.'

I hang up, and roll my eyes when I see paint smudges all over the receiver. And then I continue to work blissfully away on my painting, forgetting to eat lunch, lounging on the couch, getting lost in my Carl Jung book, then getting stuck back into painting. Before I know it, it's time for me to get ready for work.

I slip into a black lace crop top, and pull my black, silky dress over it. The one with the shoe-string straps. Lucy always goes on about us wearing something feminine. But I need to feel like myself, and keep warm on the way in, so I throw my ripped green army parka with the fur-trimmed hood over the top. Looking at myself in the bathroom mirror, I apply some black eye-liner, a touch of lip gloss, and then plenty of sandalwood oil on my wrists and neck.

I chuck my keys and purse in the front pocket of my grubby blue backpack. Flick all the lights off. Lock the front door. Wheel my bike across the crackly brown gum leaves on the lawn. Then I'm off, on my way to Harland.

8

A myriad of guilty thoughts overtake me as I roll down Darling Street. I didn't clean up the bungalow at all. I didn't leave the outside light on for Annabelle. I forgot to go to the post office yesterday and pay the phone bill.

And then Dave, like a friendly next-door neighbour, comes in through the side entrance, walks down the hall, and takes a seat on the sofa in my mind. I run through some of our funny conversations as I dodge the pot-hole on the hill and then pedal like a maniac until I get to the top—Harland on my left, the harbour in front of me.

Tiger-Lily greets me on my way down the side path. I stop momentarily and let her do her thing: her tail high in the air, her back arched, she rubs affectionately against my leg. I twinkle my fingertips through the fur on the top of her head as upbeat music from the radio in the kitchen permeates the white weatherboards and Dave's contagious laughter mixes with the muted clanging of pots and pans.

I rush towards the shed, clumsily knocking my ankle on the

pedal of my bike. Ouch! Once I'm in the hallway, Lucy makes it clear that there's no time for me to have my usual coffee and chat with Dave.

'Gatsby needs setting,' she abruptly orders, staring down at me from where she stands on a ladder in her high-heeled Mary Janes, changing the light globe inside the fringed lightshade that hangs from the high ceiling. Squishing past, I can almost see her underpants under her short, tight red dress. I'm used to her attaching little importance to the customary greeting rituals that characterise most cultures, though a simple 'hello' would have been nice.

She yells after me in a bossy tone, 'The three needs to be changed into a four, and table two needs to be reset as a three!'

'Okay!' I call back to her, knowing I'm bound to stuff this up. Three, four, two, Jesus.

Some nights, Gatsby almost feels haunted. The room has an unsettling feeling. Only when I'm in there alone, of course, when my imagination re-creates the pleasures and tribulations of 1950s Balmain East, where young working-class families occupied what is these days fast becoming a highly sought-after harbourside suburb.

I like to think about what this room must have looked like back then. Embroidered pillowcases on narrow single beds, on which blonde children laid their tired heads. Rickety, paint-chipped bedside tables covered in cream doilies and Beatrix Potter books. And there was probably an antique dressing table, on which talcum powder and a kid's brush-and-comb set were neatly placed. The smell of jam cooking on the kitchen stove would have drifted into this room, along with the sound of the father's voice rousing on the children quarrelling at the dinner table.

Lost in reverie, I set the tables. Then a crash is closely followed by an aggressive, 'I'm alright, I'm alright!'

I peek around the doorway into the hallway, where Lucy is lying on the floor. This time I *can* see her underpants. Dave approaches from the kitchen, holding a bunch of carrots.

'I just fell off! No need to freak!' Lucy avoids placing herself in a position of humiliation by making Dave and me look like worried parents, when all we are doing is calmly coming to her rescue.

'Hey Joni, I didn't realise you were here.' Dave's jovial tone contrasts with Lucy's abrasiveness like a bright moon against a dark sky. 'Let's have a coffee! Give me two secs with these carrots and I'll join you. Can you make me a flat white?'

'Sure thing.'

Lucy carries the folded ladder through the Bar Room, trying to hide her limp, too proud to admit she's actually hurt herself. I follow closely behind her. When I reach the coffee machine, I fix my eyes on it, busying myself with preparing the coffees. It's as though I'm building an invisible force field around myself and the silver machine. It's a necessary protection mechanism I often adopt when I need to shield myself from Lucy's moody outbursts. I never know if she'll be joking and friendly, or rude and demoralising.

'You need to clean the toilets after that,' she commands in a gruff tone, as though she's deliberately giving me the most demeaning task she can think of. She's just jealous that Dave wants to sit with me and talk. I know that's it—I've seen the way she looks at him.

'Coffee's up!' I yell towards the kitchen.

'Coming in a sec, Joni!'

I take a sip of my coffee, waiting for Dave to join me.

'Is Annabelle still staying at your place?' he calls out from the kitchen.

'Yeah!' I call back.

'God, you must be craving your own space.'

'I'm actually loving having her there,' I tell him.

I told Dave that Annabelle was back the day after she showed up on my doorstep. I also gave him the whole rundown on Johnny Harrison, and he couldn't believe it. He's a big fan of Johnny Harrison's music, and knows all about him.

Dave is fond of Annabelle. He met her a few times when I first started working at Harland, and I can tell he just gets her. And he understands our connection. I've told him so much about her. Some days I begin to worry that most of my conversations with people involve something that Annabelle has said or done, whether it be a recent crazy situation she found herself in, or some witty remark she made, causing a room full of strangers to become fixated on her.

I stir my coffee with a petite teaspoon. And then, with a hop and a skip, Dave's sitting next to me at the table.

'So, are Annabelle and Johnny Harrison still going strong?' he asks.

'Yeah yeah,' I tell him. 'Annabelle gives me the daily update. She talks to him most days. Can't believe you haven't seen her in the phone box up on Darling Street.'

Dave gives me a smile, and we both drink our coffees as he tells me about his day. Our conversation is cut short when the back door swings open and Lucy struts towards the bookings diary. Juliet, following close behind her in a hideous pink top hat, hovers awkwardly, dusting off tiny pieces of lint that cover the sleeves of her black velvet jacket.

Lucy does her usual assigning of sections. Tonight I get the Pines, and it's a group of eight people.

When they arrive, I give them all the once-over. Couples. Middle-class. Well-dressed. Well-groomed. Overly perfumed. They're dining at Harland tonight to celebrate a successful new business partnership. Their group is made up of the head employees of the company, and their husbands and wives. One of the ladies explains this to me as I serve their entrées, but I am too busy trying to determine if the couple seated near the door are on the verge of splitting up. The woman's body language and the bitter look on her face seem ominous. She criticises everything her partner does, and he grunts back at her.

I notice two other women at the table picking up on the whole we-hate-each-other vibe. A woman with high cheekbones and long brown hair keeps trying to encourage the breaking-up couple to make peace. Every time they speak rudely to each other, she butts in and asks them something trivial. She has an obvious lisp. Do they watch any sports? Which season do they prefer, summer or winter?

I find this mildly entertaining and, as I carry their dirty entrée plates back to the kitchen, up the haunted garden path, I forget to say my usual *Don't see a ghost, don't see a ghost.* Instead, I imagine what the lisping woman's childhood would have been like. Did she get bullied at school? Did she go to the library one day every week and see the school speech therapist? I can picture her as a schoolgirl, in long white socks, her brown hair in pigtails. Blue ribbons. I push open the back door of Harland and deliver the dirty plates to Simon in the kitchen. As per usual, he doesn't say anything, but at least he gives me a friendly smile. I give one back, then smile even more broadly as I catch Dave dancing while he plates up a couple of entrées on the steel bench.

Then Lucy appears in the doorway, preventing me from exiting the kitchen for the Bar Room. She blasts me for setting Gatsby incorrectly. Damn, I did get the numbers wrong.

By the time my group in the Pines has left, it's ten-thirty. I make a start at cleaning up after them. The wine-stained glasses, the discoloured napkins covered with lipstick wipes and coffee spills. I know the smell and sight of a table at the end of the night.

As I begin to clear the dirty wine glasses, I think to myself that there are two types of people. Those who go home and replay and over-analyse all the conversations that took place during the course of the evening, who try to decode the subtleties and nuances exchanged between the other couples. And then there are those who go home, put out the garbage, remove their make-up, say, 'That was a nice dinner,' and go to bed without a single further thought.

Once I've cleared the table, I walk up the dark path, only needing to say *Don't see a ghost* once. I enter the Bar Room, grab a glass of wine, and happily join in the chitchat that's circling around the room.

Juliet's resin jewellery is coming along nicely, but her housemate's recurring migraine headaches are unbearable for her, and Juliet doesn't know how she can help. Michael offers advice. He really is a sweet guy, sitting through Juliet's tedious anecdotes without complaint.

There has been a major shift in Lucy's mood, and she is now sharing stories with me about her recent purchases at Balmain

Market. I like this side of her. Like me, she's a collector of all things second-hand, and she goes for objects and clothing that have interesting stories behind them. Like the oak table we're sitting around right now. She bought it through the *Trading Post* from the Balmain police department. It used to sit in one of the rooms where heavy questioning took place. The conversations that would have shot back and forth over this table would be enough to inspire fifty episodes of a crime series.

It's at this point that I ask Lucy about booking the Red Room, so Annabelle can have her dinner in there with the people from *Dazed & Confused*. Lucy has no idea what *Dazed & Confused* is. I explain to her that it's pretty much the coolest fashion and music magazine in the UK, and that it's unbelievable that they want to interview Annabelle, and do a photo shoot as well. Lucy then pretends that she has heard of it, and acts all nonchalant. She checks the bookings diary, and, of course it's okay.

Great. Annabelle will be pleased.

After one drink I decide to go home. Saying my goodbyes, I catch Dave looking at me and I am taken by the sincerity of his expression. His honesty, his warm blue eyes.

'See ya Joni!' he calls to me as I turn to walk out the door. His words sound caring.

'See ya.'

The night is fresh, but not as cold as usual. The bell on my bike tinkles as I bump down the gutter, off the footpath and onto the road. I'm exhausted and make the most of the downhill run, wondering whether I'll be able to pedal my way up the hill towards my place. Almost there. Almost home. I hope Annabelle is already asleep, because I'm tired as hell and, as much as I love her, I won't be able to stay awake talking.

It's not until I'm off my bike and standing at the front door that I realise I forgot to bring my backpack home with me. There are no lights on inside my bungalow, suggesting that Annabelle is sound asleep. I don't want to wake her, but I also don't want to ride back to Harland to get my keys and purse. I'm too tired. Will I need my purse tomorrow? Probably. Maybe I can borrow money from Annabelle? This sucks. I knock lightly on the door. No answer.

I knock again. Still no answer. She's definitely asleep. I shouldn't wake her. I'm going to have to ride back to Harland and get my backpack.

Closing the gate behind me, I realise I've never ridden in to Harland at this time of night. Only home from. Nevertheless, the same thoughts occupy my mind. My painting, my group show, Annabelle's success and her love life, and Dave. And then more of Dave. His hilarious jokes, his sharp wit, his style. Well, his style's not all that great, but he's so funny. His humour makes up for his lack of style. Dave. He seems to be creeping into my mind more often than ever before. I imagine lying in his bed, waking up next to him, having tea and toast on top of white sheets. He'd be a good lover. Maybe I . . . maybe I should ask him out or something? Heaps of people get together with their friends. That is a thing.

By the time I'm out the front of Harland, I've convinced myself that I do want to ask Dave out, and try to make a move on him. I should be able to casually ask him over for lunch or whatever. Maybe to come to the market with me next weekend?

Walking my bike down the side path, I cross my fingers while still holding the handlebars. I hope he's still here. I hope he's still here. It's dead quiet, and I begin to wonder whether Lucy has locked up, and everyone has already gone home. Did they all leave straight after me? Am I that influential? Ha ha, I doubt it.

I lift my heavy legs up the back steps, and then I stop dead in my tracks. I look through the Victorian window, and there's Lucy, with her elasticised red dress hitched up around her waist. She's lying on top of someone on the staff table, and, Jesus Christ, they're having sex!

An incredibly uncomfortable feeling washes over me, but I can't stop staring. And I can't make out who she's with. I squint, noticing the black-and-white chequered material of the classic chef pants scrunched up around the victim's ankles. He is 'the victim', because I know Lucy would have pounced on her prey with full force. It's either Dave or Michael. Dave or Michael. Please don't be Dave!

And then the dotted lines connect. Dave's bike is still here. Horrified, I catch the side of his face under Lucy's long blonde hair. He's passionately kissing her on the lips.

A rush of hot, angry blood pumps through my entire body. Walking slowly back down the steps, I feel my heart beating a raging, maddened beat. How long has this been going on? Did they see me standing there? How *humiliating*. I hate Lucy!

I jump on my bike and pedal home in a ferocious mix of fury and disappointment. Now I know why Dave's been staring at me and paying more attention towards me. He feels sorry for me. He's been fucking Lucy for goodness knows how long. Why did I ever start working at Harland? I hate my life. I hate my job. I hate everything. And shit, my backpack is still in there! They're having sex in the same room as my backpack!

Tears roll down my cheeks as my anger melts into sadness. Feeling sorry for myself, pedalling my arse off up the hill, turning into my street, I stop at the gate and wipe my face. Everything sucks! Absolutely everything. I want to get a sharp knife and slash the canvas on my easel to shreds, smoke twenty cigarettes, and set Harland on fire.

9

This time, my gentle knock wakes Annabelle. She slowly opens the door. She's in a dozy daze, a half-awake state, looking like Kurt Cobain with her puffy eyes and chaotic hair. The pants of her men's stripy flannel pyjamas drag on the floor, covering her feet.

'Joni?'

'I'm so sorry, I left my keys at work.'

'Ah, no probs.'

She's so sleepy she must be unable to see my tears. After letting me in, she stumbles back onto the couch and curls up under the crocheted blanket. The heater is on, so it's warm and toasty, but not cosy enough to provide me with any form of comfort. I remove my jacket and splash my face with warm water in the bathroom, staring at myself in the mirror for a long time. My eyes are bloodshot, and black eyeliner runs down my pink cheeks. I bury my head in a towel, attempting to wipe my face clean.

With my eyes closed, the darkness feels safe, as though it's all my current internal state can cope with. I give myself some time in this cocoon, as though I'm a young child playing hide-and-seek, covering my eyes with my tiny fingers, thinking the seekers cannot see me.

After throwing the towel on the ground, I approach Annabelle's mini backpack hanging from the hook on the front door. I quietly reach in and fish around for a cigarette. My fingertips identify the smooth rectangular packet, and I'm able to slowly pull one out. Reaching in again, I push aside scrunched-up tissues and what feels like Annabelle's red lipstick, until finally I locate her lighter.

Climbing the stairs to my bed, an unlit ciggie hanging between my lips, I'm able to see myself from above, as though I'm someone else looking down upon the shambles of a twenty-one-year-old girl. Lighting the cigarette, I push open the small square window on the side wall that's level with my bed. I lie on my tummy and stick my head out into the darkness, gazing at the gum tree whose branches gently sway over Rebecca and Peter's roof. I take a drag on the cigarette, and cough and splutter smoke and spit out of my mouth, like a teenager trying a cigarette for the first time. Then I stub out the ciggie on the windowsill, hoping it creates an obvious burn mark, for which I'll get into trouble. Who am I kidding? I'm no smoker.

Exhausted by my emotions, I throw my head down onto the pillow and feel the heaviness of my limbs dissolving into the mattress. I close my eyes and exhale deeply, terrified by the thought of never being able to stop the moving image of Dave and Lucy having sex. Their tabletop pleasurefest is on loop, and each time it repeats I feel more damaged, more wounded. I toss and turn, unable to sleep, staring at the wooden ceiling for what feels like hours.

I know those wooden slats, resting up hard against each other, creating the log cabin feel I so adore. I know the circular patterns and imperfections of each slat. The ones that seem nailed in tight are the good guys, having not moved an inch in over thirty years. I'm sure that one day one of the looser ones will fall off onto my head.

And there goes my final thought before sleep—that one of the timber slats will fall off tonight, knocking me out, and relieving me of my misery. If only I could become concussed, and wake in the morning with no recollection of anything I have witnessed this evening. If only.

The familiar sounds of birds tweeting and the hum of a distant lawnmower rouse me from my sleep. I'm still in my dress from last night, and I can smell the gravy I spilt on myself while delivering the roast lamb to the group in the Pines. I lean over the edge of my bed, looking for Annabelle, and once again she's not there. I desperately need a coffee, so I head down to the kitchen, putting on my white terry-towelling bathrobe before I get the ground coffee out of the fridge.

'Hey Joni!'

It's Annabelle, backlit with a ray of sunshine as she walks through the front door. She's carrying two brown paper bags, a punnet of strawberries and a large bottle of orange juice. 'I got croissants and OJ for us!'

'Aw, thanks, that's exactly what I feel like. Let me put a pot of coffee on the stove. I had the worst night.'

'What? Let me guess. You saw Brendan at the Emerald?'

'No, thank God. I haven't been to the Emerald since . . . then. I need to get some coffee into me. Let's sit out on the verandah.'

I bring out two coffees, and Annabelle and I sit on the cane chairs in the warm morning sun.

'Thanks Joni,' Annabelle says kindly, as I hand her a hot mug of coffee just how she likes it. Milk with one.

I take a bite of my fresh, buttery croissant, and begin to open up. I start by confessing that I was beginning to feel attracted to Dave, and that I was hoping something might happen between us.

'He's gorgeous, Joni,' Annabelle throws in, making the whole situation seem even more unfortunate for me.

I cut back in, describing in detail what I witnessed through the back windows of Harland. Annabelle's face goes from hopeful to deeply sympathetic in two seconds.

'What kind of a fool am I, Annabelle?' I sip my coffee, clutching my croissant with a tense grip. 'And I feel even more stupid for becoming so distraught and worked up about it. And then . . . then I look at you, and your amazing life. You're so talented, you've toured overseas, you've got all these guys constantly falling in love with you, and your career is building and building. I'm a lost cause, Annabelle. And . . . and relationships . . .' I choke slightly on my coffee and cough. 'I can't see that happening for me. It's so depressing.' I break into what sounds like crying and laughing at the same time.

'Aw, Joni.' Annabelle gets out of her chair and crouches beside me, putting her arm around me and rubbing my back and shoulder.

'Man, I just felt so angry and awful riding home. And Lucy— I mean, she's so old and has so much baggage, and is a nightmare with a major mood disorder. And somehow she gets Dave! It was disgusting, seeing her on top of him. He deserves better than that! Plus, I thought he was showing signs that he sort of liked me. More than a friend.'

'Joni, it's going to happen for you one day, I know it will.' Annabelle holds my hand and I feel her warmth and affection. 'You're amazing, Joni. You're a beautiful, quirky little creature.'

I chuckle through my tears. 'Quirky?'

'Yes. Don't deny it. It's a compliment!' We both laugh this time.

'And your paintings are incredible. Beyond incredible! I got up this morning and I looked at the new one you're working on, and I got tears in my eyes. And the beautiful thing is, your paintings are so *you*. Your whole spirit and soul are there on the canvas. I can't paint or draw at all. I'm hopeless at art. Hopeless! I'd give anything to be able to express myself on canvas. I'm in awe of you, Joni, and the way you take a concept, or a group of thoughts and ideas, and transmute that into a visual masterpiece. And look at your place—this bungalow, and your little studio set-up, and all your things. They're so gorgeous, and you sound so happy at Harland. Well, before all of this Dave and Lucy stuff. You'll come out on top, Joni. I know you will.'

She bites into her croissant and flakes of pastry fall into her lap and all down her fluffy cardigan. I begin to feel loved and encouraged, understood and supported.

'And my life is not as great as you think, Joni. I mean, yes, I'm in love right now, and I feel like I've found my soul mate, blah, blah, blah . . . But you know me. I'm all over the place! I have my weaknesses. And Mum doesn't give a shit about me. Really, she only cares about herself and her career, and whatever new promotion she's landed. I hate having a mum in finance. It's so corporate and she has no interest in the arts. She's only come to see me play once. Once! I reckon if she heard one of my songs on the radio she wouldn't even know it was me. And Dad. He's had multiple affairs. And Mum knows about it, but doesn't say anything. It's awful. Their relationship is so . . . loveless.'

Annabelle gets up and heads back inside, still talking loudly. 'Whereas your mum works in the gallery and your dad's bookshop is so cool! And they're so in love. Still.' She comes back out onto the verandah with two glasses, and unscrews the lid of the orange juice.

'Yeah, I know, I am lucky in that way.'

Annabelle pours the juice and hands me a glass. We both take a sip, and she continues, 'Your mum understands you, and your need to create and express yourself. I've heard the way she talks to you about your work. I mean, bloody hell, she knows your influences, and how to interpret your technique and, you know, your use of colour. She gets all that. I can't imagine what it would feel like having a mother who understood me in that way.'

I sit silently, with a mental image of Annabelle's mum in her pristine grey skirt suit, sitting with her stockinged legs crossed in a board meeting. I've never really been aware of how much Annabelle longed to have parents like mine. I've never thought much about her life before we met that night at one of her first shows. And she doesn't talk much about her past. I've only been to her parents' house a couple of times. It's way out in the suburbs, and there isn't much to do out there.

I, on the other hand, grew up in the inner city. We moved around a bit, and my parents never placed much emphasis on money. I'm an only child, and Mum says I took some of my first steps on the gallery floors where she worked. Dad often tells me he taught me how to read while I sat on his lap behind the cash register at his little bookshop in Glebe. He smoked a pipe back then, and I can still remember the smell of smoke and English Breakfast tea mixed with the paperback books stacked on the wobbly shelves. My parents raised me in a world of literature and late-night dinner parties, arthouse movies and mixed media.

Mum tells me my first bedroom was a hallway. I can't remember it, but since she told me this, I've always been obsessed with hallways. 'In-Between Spaces That Take You Places' was the name of my final artwork for Painting at art school, before I started working with themes on psychology and colour, and the unspoken language and energy exchanged between people.

'Besides, Joni,' Annabelle says while opening up the strawberries, 'you don't need a boyfriend to get by in this world. You're a strong, talented, independent woman with a family who love you to bits. Let's get a video for tonight. For when you get home from work.'

'Hot chocolate and cake,' I suggest.

'That sounds perfect. Oh, and by the way, my manager told me that the photographer coming for the *Dazed & Confused* shoot is a guy from London who just split up with his girlfriend, and he's a total babe. He's going to be at Harland for the interview, and he's going to fall madly in love with you! Ha, I can see it happening!'

'As if!' Yet a small ray of hope lights up inside my body.

'Hey, let's wander up to the video shop now. Choose something for tonight.'

'Okay,' I answer, taking the last bite of my croissant.

'I'm always here for you, Joni. You know that, don't you?'

'Thanks, Annabelle. I feel so much better.'

We both get up and I offer the shower to Annabelle first. As I hear the water running, I feel guilty for feeling so jealous about her career and her fast-paced love life. She's the greatest friend I've ever had.

After I shower, I pull a second-hand dress from my clothes rack. The pink flowers on the fabric are in stark contrast with the black background, and they seem to fit my current state of mind. Last night I fell down the mountain, and this morning Annabelle has helped me climb back up to the top. I'm the vivid pink flowers; Dave and Lucy on the table are the darkness.

I rummage through the pile of jumpers on the open wooden shelf next to my clothes rack for my favourite blue falling-apart cardigan. 'I'm ready when you are,' I tell Annabelle.

'Let's go,' she says, and together we walk out the door.

On the way to the video rental shop, Annabelle tells me more about London, and about the lovely Sunday pub hot lunches, and ceramic pots with red geraniums. The black cabs that drive too fast around the tiny streets, and the crowds that plod down the steep steps, boarding the Tube with grim faces. Before we know it, we are back home with a video, hot chips and the Sunday paper.

10

I spend the rest of the day painting and chatting to Annabelle while she occupies the couch. She reads through the entire paper, offering me snippets from funny articles, dire political predictions, and what's on TV this week. And in between, she throws in further details about Johnny Harrison—who he looks like (River Phoenix), how he walks (the cool-dude swagger), how many people were at his show at The Midnight Music Hall (a thousand), and where he grew up (New Jersey). She tells me how she spoke to him on the phone yesterday, and how he told her he's bought a ticket to fly to Sydney in a couple of weeks. I'm surprised by this, but I try to act as though I'm not. Maybe Johnny really is committed to Annabelle? It's hard to know, because she's fallen in love with three people in the last eight months. The married man she had the affair with; then Ben, the bass player in Pom Pom; and now Johnny Harrison. She goes from hardcore in love, to heartbreak hotel, to newly infatuated, to hardcore in love . . . and so on. So it goes. On. Round and round. The repetitive and predictable love-cycle of Annabelle Reed.

As I paint, my eyes tire, so I give them a break, gazing over towards the kitchen. 'Oh, there's a message on my machine.'

I put down my brush and wipe my hands quickly on the scrunched-up cloth resting on the ledge of the easel. Annabelle watches me as I walk over to the answering machine and hit the playback button.

Hey Joni, it's Brendan. How's things? Um, I'm wondering if you'd like to catch a movie this afternoon, or swing by for a drink after work. I'll be at the Emerald tonight . . .

'She's not interested! She's not interested!!!' Annabelle yells over the top of Brendan's message.

Well yeah, it would be great to see you! I'll try calling you again soon. Ciao, bella!

'Urgh!' I flop down onto the couch next to Annabelle.

'God, what a weirdo,' she says. 'Waiting a whole month before he calls you. What's with that?'

And then, immediately after Annabelle's weirdo comment, the phone rings.

'You gotta get it, you gotta get it!' she yells out.

'No I don't,' I snap, in a complete panic.

'Just get it out of the way, for God's sake. Tell him you just want to be friends. Come on, do it, do it, do it!' Annabelle chants, and her cute face lights up. Her cheeks become rosy and her blonde hair bounces around as she revs me up like a cheerleader.

I give in and pick up the phone nervously. 'Hello?'

'Joni! Hi, it's me, Brendan.'

'Hi Brendan,' I answer, unenthusiastically.

'Not sure if you got my message, but I'm just wondering if you'd like to go and see a movie this afternoon. *Showgirls* is on at two o'clock in the city.'

'*Showgirls?*'

'*Showgirls?*' Annabelle laughs, and I make a big shoosh sign at her. She responds with an over-exaggerated throat-slitting gesture, and then collapses on the couch as though she's a mime artist playing dead. I can't help but start laughing.

'Is someone there?' Brendan sounds paranoid.

'Aw, it's my best friend, Annabelle. Back from London . . . well London and New York.'

'Oh, cool, I remember you telling me about her.' He pauses, and then continues, 'Yeah, so how does a movie sound?'

'Um, well, I've got heaps of work to do on my painting, and I really want to get this one finished so I can move on to some more works for the group show that's coming up.' Annabelle does the throat-slitting gesture all over again. 'And . . . I'm not sure, Brendan. I don't think we're that suited. I mean, you're a great guy and everything . . .'

Annabelle shakes her head, disapproving of my complimenting Brendan.

'I was just asking you as a friend, not like a date or anything,' he says.

'Oh sorry, I thought it sounded like a date. Good, because, yeah, I think I want to leave that side of things alone . . . if that's okay.'

'Yeah, whatever, Joni. It wasn't that great a night anyway. I mean, you're not all that experienced, and, you know, I can pick up girls really easily.'

I feel like I'm going to throw up, and I wish Annabelle could hear what he was saying. Although if she'd heard what he just said, she would have grabbed the receiver and slammed it down.

'Well, great. That's settled, then. Sorry I can't make the movie and, yeah, I'll see you around sometime.'

'Yeah, great,' Brendan says. 'Sorry to bother you. Good luck. Bye.'

Good luck? What's that supposed to mean? I hang up and stare at the mottled green tiles in the kitchen.

'All done?' Annabelle asks.

'All done,' I confirm.

'What did he say?' Annabelle looks tired, but has enough energy to maintain a high level of curiosity.

'Ah, nothing.' Returning to my easel, I feel a weight lift from my shoulders. 'It's all over. Yay.'

'Good one, Joni.' She yawns and stretches her arms out wide. 'I'm going to have a nap, is that okay?'

'Yeah sure. Go up on the bed if you want.'

I reach for the cadmium yellow deep and the cadmium scarlet, then mix both colours together on my palette. Blending the thick, almost sticky oil paints feels meditative. As I swirl the yellow with the red I smile gently, proud of myself for getting out of such an awkward situation.

After a few hours, Annabelle wakes upstairs, and startles me from my painting with her croaky: 'What time is it?'

I check the clock. 'It's four-thirty already!' I hurriedly remove as much paint from my hands as I can.

'You sure you'll be up for a video tonight?' Annabelle asks.

'Yeah, Sundays are usually pretty quiet, so I won't be home too late. Are you right for dinner?'

'Yeah, I'm just going to go up and get some pizza to take away.'

'Okay, cool.'

I keep my pink and black floral dress on, and slip into some black tights and my silver Mary Janes. My dressing table is a mess, with hair ties, ribbons, lipsticks, bangles and earrings lying here and there. I grab my hairbrush and do my hair in two loose plaits that fall gently over my collarbone. Grabbing my chunky pink plastic bangles, I gaze in the mirror, and draw satisfaction from their colour combo with my dress. Once I've put on a little make-up, I unhook my bottle-green sixties woollen coat from the back of the front door. Annabelle is still up on my bed, reading.

'I've got to go!' I call out to her. 'See you later tonight. Thanks again for listening to me and helping me out this morning. Love you!'

'Love you too.' Annabelle sits up and looks down at me. She holds her copy of John Fante's *Ask the Dust*, and I suddenly wish I was able to laze around and read instead of going to work.

My bike's handlebars are ice cold. When I reach into the pockets of my coat, I am pleasantly surprised to find my black woollen gloves, one in each pocket. As I wheel my bike out and open the gate, I notice how weird it feels to be leaving the house with no keys and no backpack. I'm such a loser for forgetting to bring them home last night. Thank god Annabelle was able to let me in and lend me money today. My feet push down on the pedals, and the cool evening air begins to chill my cheeks.

As I swerve around the corner onto Darling Street, I notice how good I feel compared to late last night. I've gotten over my anger and humiliation since catching Lucy and Dave in the act. And I think I'm slowly coming to terms with the fact that Dave's taken, and that it's unlikely he and I will ever be more than friends. Also, I'm rid of my worries about how to tell Brendan

I'm not interested in him. I grip my glove-covered fingers tightly around the handlebars as I begin to pedal faster, along the valley, and up the hill towards Harland.

The red brake-lights of a car reverse-parking up ahead remind me of an installation I saw at an opening recently. I love the look of red lights on cars at dusk, when the sky still has a hint of blue. There's something intensely beautiful about red. It is by far my favourite colour. Love, lust, desire, heat, sexuality, romance, rage, danger.

As I wheel my bike up onto the footpath in front of Harland, Tiger-Lily runs to me and rubs against my leg. I take a deep breath, trying to convince myself that I am not jealous or hurt in any way after seeing Dave and Lucy having sex last night. It's beginning to feel real. Like a genuine feeling of acceptance. Although I'm worried that when I see them both, this feeling may very quickly crumble into humiliation and hopelessness.

11

Simon is sitting at the staff table when I walk through the back doorway. He's sipping on a latte, smoking a ciggie. His relaxed, slouchy body is hunched over the table, and his long, dark blond hair looks like it hasn't been washed for weeks. He wears chunky silver Celtic rings, and a black leather necklace falls halfway down his hollow chest, weighed down by a mysterious-looking bronze pendant. It's sort of like a cross, or a hammer. I can't quite tell, and I don't really want to go in closer to get a better look for fear of being taken out by his smelly BO.

Every T-shirt he's ever worn to Harland has a hole in it. Actually, most have multiple holes. I don't think he does much during the day. If he does, he certainly doesn't share it with us. He's possibly cruising through a lazy phase in his life. Or maybe this is Simon's forever disposition. Who knows. Tonight, his lips look cracked and dry.

'Hi Simon,' I smile, and he nods a *hello*, a nod that looks awkwardly like he's bowing down to me, ready to do whatever I say.

Dave is in the kitchen, and pokes his head around the corner playfully, a dirty tea towel flung over his shoulder. 'Hey Joni!'

'Hi Dave.'

Mmmm. I feel okay. But only okay.

'I'm just finishing up this béchamel, and then I'll come out and join you for a coffee.'

'Okay, sure. I'll get the coffees started.'

I bury my head in the coffee machine. I realise that this is becoming a bit of a habit, but I don't want to get into boring small talk with Simon, so I behave like the shy aunt at the family Christmas dinner who keeps busy doing the washing up all night so she doesn't have to talk to anyone. I look down at my coat, and it suddenly feels too over-the-top. I felt confident enough to wear it when I left the house, but now I wish I'm wearing my blue cardigan, or a big grey trench to hide behind.

As I'm frothing the milk, I turn and take a long look at the staff table where last night's action took place. Yuck! Although, actually, it was Dave's bare bum that was lying on that table. But, yeah—yuck! That disgusts me, which makes me question just how attracted to Dave I really am. I'm just desperate. But obviously not as desperate as Lucy.

My nerves overtake my thoughts when I hear the sound of the screen door opening. It's got to be her. It's got to be Lucy. My stomach tenses up, and then a long purple terry-towelling skirt covered in cheap-looking white lace becomes visible as the back door swings inwards. It's Juliet, and she exhales a loud, 'Hi Joni! Hi Simon!' before throwing her black backpack on the floor. She sits at the table and stretches her arms out, slowly rubbing her hands all over the exact area where Dave's bum was last night.

She's wearing a lime-green turban covered in a ladybird print, and bright orange lipstick.

Her outfit is beyond atrocious. It's a mismatched colour palette that hurts my head when I look at her. I begin to wonder whether she raided her niece's dress-up box before coming to work. But I must admit I do find her quite entertaining. She is nice, she is sorta funny. She's never really unkind to anyone. I do like her. And besides, I'd rather surround myself with unusual people than mingle with complete bores.

'What a day,' she begins, and I know this is the intro to a long whinge. 'I just had to move all my furniture out of my room because the landlord is painting it tomorrow. God, so heavy! I have so much crap!'

'Oh, that's weird,' I tell her, pouring the frothed milk into Dave's coffee. 'Usually they just get you to drag it all into the middle of the room, and then they cover it and they can still get to all the walls and ceiling.'

'Well, he told me they need it all out. I think they're sanding the floors as well. Can you do me a giant favour and make me a coffee? Seeing as you're there?'

'Sure.'

I start on Juliet's latte as Dave walks into the room with his usual enthusiastic energy. He pretty much ignores Juliet and Simon, and asks me all about my day. I fill him in with the details that seem appropriate—hot chips, catching up with Annabelle, and painting. While I do this, I look at his semi-ugly, overly bushy eyebrows, his unattractive paper-thin lips, and his slight, unmanly body. Anything I can see that will help me turn my back on my desire for a romantic relationship with him. Anything that will assist me in reverting to having a feeling of contentment in just being good friends with him.

'You left your backpack here last night,' he says, after his first sip of coffee.

'I know. Annabelle was home, so she let me in. How was your day?'

Dave tells me that he slept in and then wandered up to the Emerald and had a few lunch-time beers. Because he had heaps of unpacking and prepping to do here, he came in around two o'clock.

'Nice.' I stir my coffee slowly with a spoon.

Dave continues. 'Lucy met me at the Emerald.'

'Oh,' I reply. *She fucking slept over at your house and you both walked up there together, you liar.* I try to think *Who cares?* but I can't kid myself—I kind of do care.

I hand Juliet her coffee and sit beside Dave, and then Lucy waltzes in through the back door in a sheer black silk top and a gorgeous flowing black velvet skirt. Her blonde locks fall casually around her shoulders, one side pinned up with a clip decorated with a crimson rose. She smells of what I recognise as Yves Saint Laurent's dark classic: Opium, a perfume my art teacher in high school wore. Lucy's got the Bette-Midler-in-*Beaches* look about her tonight, in a good way—glamorous, but dishevelled at the same time. I can see why Dave has fallen under her spell.

'Hi Joni, hi Jules,' she purrs through her red lips. 'Nice coat, Joni,' she adds, and I instantly feel glad that I chose to wear it this evening. I like it when Lucy likes me. I watch her run her slender fingers down the open page of the bookings diary as she checks how many people we have in this evening.

'We've got a quiet night tonight, girls. No one in the Red Room.

No one in the Pines. Juliet, would you mind doing a proper dust and clean in the Red Room and the Pines?'

'Sure,' Juliet answers, through a milk moustache from her frothy coffee. What is she, five?

'Joni, we'll cover Lillibon and Gatsby, and maybe do a bit of a clean-up in here.'

'Okay.' I take note of her orders while finishing my coffee.

'I've got some insanely great falafels for dinner tonight, girls,' Dave tells us, taking our empty coffee cups into the kitchen.

And then Michael arrives, sheepishly saying a soft hello to everyone.

'Mikey boy!' Dave calls out from the kitchen, reappearing seconds later with a tray of falafels, tabouli and pita bread. He's gifted at drawing a gang together, with his inclusive, lively disposition. Michael sits, and then Lucy joins us all around the table.

We happily begin eating the non-French meal—a nice change from the creamy, buttery food we usually get. I have to say, the menu here is killer, but a little monotonous when we have it night after night.

Juliet talks to Michael nonstop, with her mouth full. I hear the re-cap of her furniture lifting, and how she's left it all on the balcony out the front of her house, ready for the painter to arrive tomorrow morning. She has three huge bits of parsley stuck in her teeth, and Michael doesn't say anything. He just listens.

Lucy looks over at Juliet and scrunches her face up. 'You're not wearing that ladybird scarf thing tonight, are you? It doesn't look quite right with your purple skirt. The colours . . . together.' She waves her fingers around over the top of Juliet's head.

'I was thinking I might wear it. But that's cool, I don't have to.'

Juliet removes the lime green ladybird turban, and her hair looks so greasy I can understand why she was covering it.

'Great!' Lucy seems pleased to have made a suggestion that was accepted with no answering back. She heads out the back door, and returns with a pile of neatly chopped firewood in her arms.

I take off my coat and hang it on the hat rack, reach for my apron, and glance at the open page of the bookings diary; I check how many are coming, when they are expected, and where they are to be seated. Juliet puts on a Serge Gainsbourg CD, and his smooth sultry music wafts through the rooms of Harland, weaving around the legs of the antique tables and chairs.

Tiger-Lily jumps up on the back window ledge and rubs her back against the glass. I wander outside and give her a pat, hearing her soft purr travel through the cold, crisp air. Her water bowl is almost empty, so I refill it, then head back inside, absorbing the warmth coming from the newly lit fires.

At six-thirty the first couple arrives and I seat them in Gatsby. They look like they're in their twenties, and they tell me they're celebrating their two-year anniversary. The handsome Asian man has slick black hair and he carries a single red rose with a pink velvet ribbon tied around the stem. The woman has a particular nervous giggle that she repeats after each sentence she utters. It's quite captivating, and I can see her partner gazing lovingly at her freckled face whenever she talks. Her ginger hair is tied back, and her fingernails are painted red. I seat them near the fire, and they immediately reach over the menus I've placed in front of them, and hold hands.

They have an intimate connection. A warm energy floats between them. I can't imagine they'd ever fight with each other.

I guess that she's a secretary and he's a doctor. Or maybe it's the other way around? I can tell their house or apartment would be spotless, minimal, clean.

I ask them both if they'd like something to drink, telling them the wine list is on the back page of the menu. As I wait for a response, I glance into the Red Room, and see that Juliet is already in there with a feather duster. I catch sight of her lifting each urn off the shelf, one by one, and dusting it in a bubbly fashion, as though she's a contented housewife from the 1950s.

Lucy seats the next group of people in Lillibon, and when I go in there to check on them I'm fascinated by how beautiful they are. I notice myself standing taller, slowing down my movements, trying to look as well-to-do as possible. They are a handsome family of five, all with the same blue eyes and curly hair, although the dad's hair is only slightly wavy. The two sisters and brother, who look like they're all in their twenties, share in-jokes with each other, while the mum opens beautifully wrapped presents, all tied with fancy bows that match the wrapping paper. She reads each card as she opens it, ahhing and giving thanks, getting up to hug each of her adult children in turn. It's a little sickening, how happy they are.

I begin to imagine what their dark secrets might be. I mean, everyone has them, buried deep down. Maybe the brother's business is about to go bankrupt, but he would never dare tell his parents. Maybe the father killed the family dog with rat poison but lied to them all, saying she must have walked away to die peacefully in the bushland that surrounds their house. The mum had a baby with her English teacher when she was eighteen and put him up for adoption, and she's never even told her husband; but next year the adopted boy will track down the mother and the whole family will fall apart. Then they'll discover her secret gambling problem. Soon after, the dad will come out of the closet, and admit he's been having an affair with another man for three years.

This is all possibly a little far-fetched, but I'm bored senseless if I don't conjure up scenarios like this. I wait for their drink orders, twiddling the tie of my apron with my left hand, holding a notepad and pen in my right.

Lillibon is a cute little room, named after Lucy's grandmother. The ivy wallpaper that covers all four walls is faded in the corners, some sections torn and discoloured with what looks like water damage. I love these imperfections. The torn edges remind me of the fragile outlines of countries on a large map, like the ones that hung in my primary school classrooms. There's a cuckoo clock hanging on the wall, and its non-stop *tick-tock* can be heard every second, like a repetitive, robotic heartbeat. On the hour, two wooden doors above the clock face open up, and a little boy and girl spring out each time the cuckoo calls. I often hear it throughout the restaurant, whether I'm re-setting Gatsby or taking orders into the kitchen.

By the time the two-year-anniversary couple leave Gatsby, there are only seven people left finishing their meals and sipping their wine. Lucy calls me into the Bar Room, and I sit down at the staff table in front of a large pile of white napkins. I begin to fold them one by one as Lucy dusts and rearranges the liquor bottles and coffee cups on the shelf near the coffee machine. She begins to talk to me as though a switch has been flicked, and she's finally decided she can trust me.

12

'My ex-husband is a piece of work,' Lucy tells me, taking down the liquor bottles from the shelf. 'Have I ever told you about him?'

'No.'

'We met when I was twenty-seven, in Paris. I was living in my apartment in Montmartre, and we'd stay up late drinking in smoky bars, dancing at all the cool clubs in Pigalle, and then we'd stumble home together.' She pauses, then continues. 'Those were the days. Our salad days.'

She places a full bottle of vodka on the bench, and I can see her getting lost in this enjoyable slice of her past.

'God, I remember we'd trip up the stairs like two drunken lunatics, laughing out loud, getting yelled at by the old woman in the downstairs apartment. And then we'd have great sex on the Persian rug in the living room.'

She turns her head and stares at nothing in particular, and I get a French version of *Breakfast at Tiffany's* in my mind. Then I notice Lucy's facial expression quickly change, as though a storm has blown over.

'He was such a prick!' she yells. 'An absolute bastard! If I saw him now, I'd spit in his face!' She begins to slam the liquor bottles on the bench, one by one, giving them a stern wipe down, as though they're children who have misbehaved.

'Was he Australian?' I ask hesitantly, frightened she'll tell me off.

'Yeah, he grew up in Sydney, which is why we settled back here. He was in France *en vacances*—holidaying with friends, who by the way were all obnoxious young businessmen. But he stood out, you know? I was working in a patisserie near my apartment. I didn't need the money because my parents had loads, but I needed something to do with my time. Working at the patisserie helped keep me out of trouble. My boss let me rearrange the window display, and bring in a lot of cake stands and china plates that I'd collected from all my weekends spent foraging around at the Montreuil flea market. We fought like crazy, me and my boss, but I loved it, and it's what made me want to run my own place.'

'So how did you meet, um . . .'

'Damian?'

'Yeah.'

'He started coming into the patisserie every morning to get his coffee. He was so handsome back then. Like Jean-Paul Belmondo, you know, the lead guy in that film you love, *À bout de souffle. Breathless.* He'd hand me the money, and the way his top teeth bit his bottom lip . . . awww, it killed me! He was so gorgeous. And he was always half asleep—with bed hair, and little sheet creases on his face. He'd try to order in French, getting it all completely wrong. I'd never really heard an Australian accent before and I could not believe how adorable he sounded.'

Lucy pauses and smiles, wiping the bench gently. Then storm number two blows in. 'I can't believe I got sucked in!' Her tone of voice is brutal. 'Worst mistake of my life!'

I want to ask her what went wrong. Why did they separate? Why does she hate him so much? What's it like being divorced? I'm too afraid, though, so I sit silently, continuing to fold the white napkins as neatly as possible, pressing down on each fold with my fingertips. Then, to my surprise, she continues to reveal more, of her own free will.

'Il a eu une aventure.'

I don't know what she's talking about when she says it in French. 'What does that mean?'

'He cheated on me with an older woman,' she says, with disgust. 'He was always running after skirts. And I know I'm . . . hard to live with, up and down. I admit all that. But he wanted kids, and I was not able to give him that.'

'What do you mean—you don't like children?'

She hesitates before she goes further. I can tell she's beginning to wonder whether it's a good idea, telling me her personal history. At this point one of the curly-haired sisters from Lillibon comes into the Bar Room. Her cheeks are flushed and she giggles while asking for the bill.

I leave the napkins on the staff table and place the torn-out page from my order pad on a rosy saucer, adding some after-dinner mints on top. As soon as I arrive at their table, the dad lays a wad of cash on the saucer. I see them out the door, wishing them all the best. As I do this, my mind is sifting through all the information Lucy's been telling me. I'm eager to get back into the Bar Room and hear more about her failed marriage, and her lack of interest in having children.

I clear Lillibon as quickly as I can, taking all the dirty dessert plates, glasses and coffee cups in to Simon. Dave's busy cleaning out the fridges below the bench. Michael must have been sent home, and I haven't seen Juliet for a while. Her bag is not on the floor, so Lucy must have sent her home early too.

I settle back in front of the pile of napkins, turning to see Lucy giving the coffee machine a good clean. She's shifted it right over to the other side of the bar area and, after polishing the top and sides, she gives the bench another wipe down. She smiles at me as I get back to my folding, and when she picks up from where she left off, my body relaxes as though I've just pressed Play on a video that was paused mid-movie.

'I do like kids. I did want to have a baby,' she confesses. 'Quite desperately.'

I stay silent.

'I was diagnosed with very severe endometriosis when I was sixteen.'

'What's endometrio . . .'

'Endometriosis. It's a disease.' She looks me directly in the eyes. 'You know this is hard for me to talk about. I don't tell this to everyone.'

I return her gaze, feeling scared and privileged at the same time.

She carries on. 'A lot of women have it, but you don't hear about it much.' She unexpectedly adds, 'Marilyn Monroe had it.'

'Oh. What . . . what happens to you if you have it?'

'You get incredibly bad pain with your period, like I'm talking horrifically bad. Imagine there are knives stabbing into your uterus for days at a time, every month. It's a relentless, agonising feeling. That's how it was for me anyway, because I had it really bad.'

I hardly know anything about the female anatomy, let alone strange-sounding diseases. I'm so intrigued I can't help but begin to ask one of the many questions that are welling up in my mind. 'I knew Marilyn Monroe had a miscarriage, but—'

Lucy abruptly cuts in. 'But you didn't know that one of the reasons she could never get to the studio on time was probably because she was lying in her bed in excruciating pain. You didn't know that, did you, Joni!'

I am once again in frightened mode. Lucy makes me feel like my lack of knowledge of Marilyn Monroe's health problems is a crime for which I should be punished.

'Seriously, I used to take a heavy combination of painkillers, and I'd still have no relief. I remember we were in the change rooms at school, getting ready to play a game of football, like . . . ah, you call it soccer, yeah, round ball?'

'Yeah.'

'So my team . . . we were in the change rooms, and I had such, such bad pain, I was sweating all over.' Her eyes widen, and her speech quickens. 'I was trying to stand up to find the teacher to tell her I wasn't well enough to play, but I couldn't get up. Then I started hearing all these echoing voices, bouncing back and forth against the tiled walls. Everything went blurry, and then *bang*!'

Lucy claps her hands together on the *bang*, as though we're sitting around a campfire and she's delivering the dramatic punchline to a scary story. 'My head hit the wooden seat, and I was out like a light. I ended up in hospital on morphine, and I thought I was dying.'

'Fuck, that's so intense.'

'And then it got even worse.' Lucy looks towards the kitchen, and I imagine she's probably checking to see if Dave is listening

97

in. He must be busy cleaning away, oblivious to what we're talking about out here.

So Lucy continues, turning down the volume. 'Don't forget this was me when I was sixteen.' She moves closer towards me, and lowers her voice even further. 'I was already sleeping around. Even though it hurt so much when I did it. I mean . . . I don't really want to go into that.'

'What . . . what do you mean—hurt?'

'Your whole insides are screwed, so when you screw, it's agony.'

We both smile.

'So do you still have all the pain now? You never—'

Lucy cuts in sternly. 'My endometriosis became so bad they had to schedule me in to have an operation so surgeons could remove some of the growths from my body.'

'Growths?'

'Well . . .' She takes a deep breath. *Have I shared too much personal information with Joni? Should I go on?* These are the questions I think she is asking herself. She gazes out the back window and rests her eyes on Tiger-Lily, who's curled up in the cane chair on the verandah. Then, she decides to go on.

'Small parts of the lining of your uterus end up in other areas of your pelvis, and then they begin to bleed. A lot of the pain you experience is from your organs absorbing that blood. Isn't that so sad and awful, for any girl. For any woman.' Lucy adjusts the flower in her hair and runs her fingers under her breasts, as though she's convincing herself that she's extremely attractive and sexy, even though she's had to live through what sounds like a horrifically unsexy time. In convincing herself, she also convinces me. She is stunning. Crazy, but overwhelmingly attractive.

'I thought God was torturing me for being such a rebellious girl,' she tells me. 'For sleeping around—skipping class. I became so depressed.' Lucy begins to turn around all the liquor bottles she's placed back on the shelf, so the labels face the front. 'And right before my operation I collapsed again. Maman called the ambulance and I was rushed into emergency. I remember bumping down the cobble-stoned streets of Montmartre in the back of the ambulance, the siren blaring as I drifted in and out of consciousness. Then the doctors discovered that my blood was thick with infection that had originated somewhere in my internal parts.' She turns to face me, rubbing her hands over her pelvic area, then drops her arms. 'It had spread throughout my entire body.'

I move the piles of folded napkins to the side, and start polishing the cutlery. I look up at Lucy. I'm so blown away by the fact that she's chosen to reveal all these intimate details to me.

'And then came emergency surgery. I was like a sick puppet hanging from a string, out of it on morphine, and God knows what else. They wheeled me into the operating theatre, and I overheard the nurses saying there was a chance they would need to give me a full hysterectomy. Then a tall doctor in a white coat with black hair and silver glasses leaned over my face and said, "*J'espère que tu ne comptes pas avoir d'enfants.*"'

'What does that mean?'

Lucy slows down her speech, and translates the words: 'I hope you're not planning to have children.'

She has stopped her cleaning and clearing and is now sitting on the bench, looking solemn. She pours herself some red wine, crosses her legs and holds the glass in her fine fingers. I realise

I'm in awe of her. Her beauty, her darkness, her hard edge, and her tragic teenage health problems. I feel so honoured that she has brought me into her world. She's beginning to feel more like a friend than my boss.

She takes a sip of her wine, and says with an air of disgust, 'I cannot get those heartless words out of my head. Of course I'd thought about having children! Of course I hoped to be a mother! When I was little, I'd always look for new babies in my street and I'd approach their mothers, asking them if I could look after their newborn babies. Joni, I adored children so much. It was all I wanted. My own baby.'

I wasn't expecting to hear this. Not from Lucy. I had no idea she was the type of woman who longed for children. 'And . . . and then what happened?'

'They took out my fucking uterus. And they had to take out both my ovaries as well.' Lucy sculls her full glass of wine, and pours herself another. 'You want one?'

'What, a baby?'

'No, a glass of wine.' She smiles. 'And a baby. You want one of those?'

I hardly know how to answer. 'Yeah, I'll have a glass.' I take a deep breath. 'I . . . I can't imagine having babies. I don't even have a boyfriend. I mean, maybe. Maybe as I get older I'll think about it. Probably. I can't really tell, I'm only twenty-one.'

'Oh, I knew I wanted one when I was five,' Lucy admits, before taking another sip of her wine.

'It must have been so hard for you.'

'Joni, my worst nightmare had come true. I mean, out of all the things that could have gone wrong for me, this was by far the worst I could imagine.'

She licks her lips, swinging her legs in time to Serge Gainsbourg's 'Bonnie and Clyde'.

'I've accepted it all now,' she says, looking at the floor. 'But . . . but back then, I slowly started to spiral downwards. After I'd healed from the surgery, I went on to study a bachelor degree in history, but I had to drop out because I fell into a deep depression. I don't think I had ever really dealt with how traumatic my health situation had been, and I was beginning to feel like life was not worth living if I couldn't have a baby. Then I started hanging out with this maniac girl, Stephanie. And . . . I don't know how it happened, but I ended up on the street, and I joined Stephanie and started working as a stripper in a dodgy club in Pigalle. I was pretty much homeless. Well, for a little while.'

I don't know what to say. It's so much to take in.

'I basically went through menopause when I was nineteen. Can you think of anything worse! A menopausal nineteen-year-old girl who is also pumped up with teenage hormones. I was a fucking mess, Joni. A mess.'

'Why were you going through menopause? My mum's just started going through that now.'

'It's what happens when you get your lady parts ripped out. Well—uterus and ovaries.'

'Man, Lucy, that must have been such a difficult time for you.'

'It was. The doctors said I was one of the youngest girls they'd operated on with endometriosis who had to have a full hysterectomy. It doesn't usually happen to women until they're in their twenties or thirties. But lucky me, hey,' she says, sarcastically.

'And wow, you were a stripper? What was that like?' I am very drawn to this part of her story. It's so B-grade movie, so Courtney Love.

'Ah, that was . . . shall I say, rough going. Kind of fun, but so degrading. I'm so glad I finally cleaned myself up.'

I pick up my wine with both hands, wrapping my fingers around the glass, resting my elbows on the table.

'A few years later I got the job at the patisserie, and then I met Damian. He was the bright light in my life, I'm telling you. After a few years of him living with me in my apartment, he convinced me to move to Sydney with him. It worked for me, because I felt like settling in Sydney was a good way for me to leave my past behind me, and start anew.'

I think about what Dave told me about Lucy's parents both dying in a car accident when they came to visit her in Australia, but I don't dare bring it up. What a tragic life she's had! I suddenly feel so sympathetic towards her, excusing all her rude and irrational behaviour.

'Anyway. That's why Damian left me—because I could not have children.'

'Did he know that before you got married, that you couldn't get pregnant?'

'That's the other big mistake I made in my life. I didn't tell him. I just said to him I was desperate to have a family with him, because I knew how much he wanted kids. He would not have married me had he known I was without a uterus. But I'm a compulsive liar, you know that.'

That makes me wonder whether she's lying or telling the truth now. And also, Damian would have eventually found out. What was she thinking?

'And then I told Damian all about it, after we'd been trying for a baby for three years. I'd been pretending I still had my period, telling him it was so light, I hardly bled, and he believed me. That's also when I found out he'd been having an affair for a long time. Then he walked out on me, and a few months later he was fucking a woman who worked in his office, and surprise, surprise, she got knocked up. Thank god I was already working here. If I didn't have Harland, I would not have been able to go on.'

Once again I don't know what to say. I stand up and move the piles of folded napkins, placing them under the bench. Then Lucy says quietly, 'I saw you watching us last night.'

My face heats up, and I can tell I've gone bright red. My heart races, and I look down at the floor.

'Dave and I have been together for quite a while now. We didn't really want to tell any of you because . . . I don't know, we thought it could interfere with work stuff.'

I slowly build up the courage to speak. 'I was just coming to get my backpack. I left it here last night. I . . . I didn't come in because—'

'It's alright, Joni. You don't have to explain yourself.'

'What about you kissing Juliet the other night?'

'That was just a bit of fun. And by the way, I'm not thirty-eight. I'm forty-three. Don't tell anyone.' She winks, and heads out of the Bar Room into the hallway.

I sit down on my chair at the table again, leaning my shoulders on the chair back. I slowly exhale. What an amazing amount of information to process. I can't wait to tell Annabelle all of this.

13

When Dave comes into the Bar Room to join us for a knock-off drink, I look at him in an entirely new way. I'm pretty sure he's in his early twenties, like twenty-two or twenty-three. Actually, I'm certain he's twenty-three, because he told me at the karaoke night at the Emerald a few months ago.

Jesus, he's dating a forty-three-year-old woman! Holy-b-moly! And he probably thinks Lucy's only thirty-eight, because I clearly remember she told us all that on the same karaoke night. It was right after she'd sung an extraordinary rendition of 'Like a Virgin', while oblivious to the fact that I still was one. And after this evening's confession—the *compulsive liar* one—I doubt very much that she has told Dave her true age.

Maybe I'm too hung up on things like this. Does it really matter if your partner is almost twice your age? How weird—going to visit a baby boy in hospital when you're twenty, thinking, *You could be my future husband!* Ah dear. Maybe I should start looking at older men? My probability of finding a boyfriend would increase. That would be a plus.

Suddenly Juliet bursts into the Bar Room, cutting short my contemplation of seeking a boyfriend in his forties. 'Done!' she cries out in a high operatic sing-song.

Weird. I thought she'd left already. Maybe Lucy sent her outside to clean the windows, or tidy up the firewood. Juliet's unattractive hand with its bitten fingernails reaches for a wine glass on the top shelf. She helps herself to a bottle of sauvignon blanc from the bar fridge and, with a quick pour, fills her glass, splashing wine over the rim. At the same time, Lucy slips into the Bar Room from the hallway, carrying a saucer with a pile of cash on it, which must be from the last couple who were dining in Gatsby.

'Large tip here, ladies,' she announces. Her make-up is still flawless, her posture perfect. She draws attention to herself without even having to try. I smile at her tenderly, with a newly formed sense of fondness.

Dave catches me doing this, and gives me a warm grin. I throw him a smile, feeling more at ease with the idea of him and Lucy being a couple. Then I begin to wonder if he heard Lucy's and my whole conversation. I try to tell him telepathically: *Don't worry, her secrets are safe with me.* Well, me and Annabelle.

'Hey Joni, can I get you to do the till tonight?' Lucy asks. 'Sorry, my love, I just get a bit over it sometimes.'

'No worries,' I tell her. It's another way in which she's displaying her trust in me, allowing me to count her money at the end of the night.

I walk up the hallway to where the gorgeous antique cash register sits on the sideboard. I pull down on the cold gold lever that sticks out the side. A ding sounds as the tray shoots out, stopping with a jolt and a jingle of the coins. I begin to count, and then I'm distracted by the sound of Simon saying, 'Time for me to grab a beer.'

I look over my shoulder, and see him walking slowly through the kitchen doorway into the Bar Room, untying his apron and running his wet pruney hands through his sweaty hair. Yuck! His Pearl Jam T-shirt is grease-stained and there are large sweat patches around the armpit area. He picks his nose with little to no effort at hiding it from everyone in the Bar Room, wiping his booger on his baggy skate pants. Ewww. Remind me to never, ever date a dish-hand. Climbing into bed with that stench! I bet Simon doesn't wash his sheets for months. His pillowcase would stink like unwashed hair, and the gravy and grease he absorbs through his puffy wet hands in the sink all night. I bet his room smells like foot odour and BO.

He turns towards me and notices that I'm watching him. I fabricate a friendly smile, which he seems to accept as genuine. I don't know if he has much going on upstairs. Now I feel terrible. My judgemental thoughts are mellowed by the arrival of my default setting: sympathy. Possibly not my default setting at all times; tonight, though, after sitting through Lucy's verbal memoir, my sympathy dial has been turned up. Not sexually. Not for Simon! Ahhh, gross!

After counting the money, I pull up a chair at the staff table. My eyes follow Juliet's path to the bar fridge. She refills her glass right up to the top, making the most of Lucy's generous 'as many drinks as you like' rule for knock-offs, and then she plonks herself down next to Dave. After some surface-level small talk, she and Dave begin a Top Five Films to and fro.

Dave starts with *Delicatessen*, one of my favourite French

films, and I'm instantly reminded that Annabelle and I hired *Reality Bites* on video, and that I need to get going so I can a) tell Annabelle all about Lucy, and b) start watching one of my own personal faves. I start gathering my things together, worried that I'll overhear Juliet's Top Five list, and that some of her favourite films will be the same as mine. If so, I'll start questioning my own taste.

I lift my green coat off the hook on the hatstand and place my hand on Dave's shoulder in a friendly, non-flirty way. Dave and Lucy make a good couple, a good *secret* couple. I'm glad nothing ever happened between me and Dave. I love our friendship just the way it is, and things at Harland would have gone totally weird if we'd gotten together. As I pick up my backpack, I wonder when Dave and Lucy will tell the others about their romance. I don't want to interfere with that. They'll work it out, I'm sure.

'Bye everyone,' I say loudly, walking towards the back door.

Lucy gives me a special farewell. 'Bye Joni,' she says. 'So nice talking to you tonight. Have a great day tomorrow.'

She kisses me once on each cheek, then I wave towards Simon and Juliet, not really caring if they see me.

The cold air hits my face as soon as I open the back door. Such a stark contrast from the indoors to the outside—from Harland, with its warm glowing interior, to the quiet darkness of the garden path. *Don't see a ghost, don't see a ghost,* my inner voice repeats, as I descend the rickety wooden stairs. At the shed now, I hold onto the handlebars of my bike, and pull it away from Dave's. I do up the top button on my green coat, take my gloves out of the pockets, and pull them on tightly. The side path is dimly lit by the honeyed glow that seeps through the curtains hanging in the window of the house next door. There's no ghost loitering here. Perhaps it's all to do with darkness—where there is light, there is no ghost.

Once I'm out on the street, I climb onto my bike seat and slowly pedal down the centre of the bitumen. My mind is full to the brim with Lucy Bourdillon, Lucy Bourdillon. What a woman! Her life story is that of a character from a daytime soap. I feel so inspired to paint! What is it about complex females that makes me feel so alive, and capable of churning out hundreds of artworks? And what a turnaround for her to confide in me like that! I love her. Love her to bits. Poor thing, with all those health problems. And how crazy—her stripping and living on the street!

I reckon she'll invite me over to her place one day soon. Oh my god, her house must be amazing! An assortment of wild and wonderful artefacts from all over France and Europe. Dave has told me she lives in a huge sandstone house on the waterfront. No wonder he's gotten together with her! Scrambled eggs on toast, sitting on the upstairs balcony overlooking the pool. Oh, and the Harbour Bridge and Opera House. And she'd have a boat, I bet. Like a big yacht. What a life! Davey boy, you have scored, my friend. Big time.

I look up and my thoughts fade as I get closer to the Emerald. There it stands, high and mighty on the top of the hill. As I ride past, a woman in a navy duffel coat walks out onto the footpath from the main door of the pub, allowing the classic mix of golden oldies hits and jovial conversation to escape momentarily.

Turning off Darling Street, the *clinkity-clack* of my bike

becomes more noticeable, and then I burst into a joyful smile. Yes! I didn't think about Brendan when I passed the Emerald! And I didn't think about him the whole time I was at Harland tonight! Is this confirmation that the whole losing-my-virginity episode is officially over? I think so.

Continuing to smile, I pull up at the gate that leads to where my bungalow is nestled. The wood palings of the gate are full of splinters, so I'm always cautious when I unhook the rusty metal latch. The fallen twigs from the large gum crackle underfoot as my bicycle wheels roll over the patchy lawn. I park my bike and with an upbeat step I light-heartedly make my way up the stairs.

As I open the front door and remove my backpack from my shoulders, Annabelle startles me. 'Joni.'

'Hey!' I lean in to hug her.

She's in her jammies. The video is already in the machine, and she's baked a chocolate cake and placed it on my one-and-only cake stand in the centre of the table.

'Aww, man, that looks amazing,' I tell her.

I unload all my stuff—coat, keys, backpack—and take a quick shower. Once I'm in my jimmy jams, Annabelle cuts me some cake and I tell her all about Lucy. She's enthralled, but she does interrupt me every now and then with 'Oh, that's like me and Johnny', or 'Johnny told me a story like that'. She's very obviously obsessed with him. Fixated.

After our video, I climb the ladder stairs and snuggle in under the covers. I look down, and Annabelle is curled up on the couch, looking so pretty with her bleached fluffy hair.

'Do you ever think about whether or not you want kids?' I ask her. 'Have we ever talked about that?'

'Oh god, yeah,' she answers. 'I'd definitely have them with Johnny.'

'Really?' I answer, quite surprised.

'I wanna be like Mia Farrow,' she tells me, as I roll back to stare up at the wooden panels of my ceiling.

'Like adopt kids?' I ask.

'Adopt, *and* have my own.'

'Wow, like a big family?'

'Totally. And I want to have kids when I'm young.'

'Really?' I know I sound shocked, but I can't remember ever . . .

'We've talked about this already—'member? Ages ago.'

'Oh, yeah. I remember you saying you wanted lots of kids, but I can't remember you saying you wanted to adopt some as well.'

'How 'bout you? You still unsure?'

'Think so.'

'What—think you're unsure, or think you want some?'

'I don't know,' I reply, honestly. 'I think I'd need to meet someone and fall in love with them before I made my mind up.'

We lie there in silence, my eyes following the swirling patterns in the timber up above.

'I'm really tired,' Annabelle says, yawning. 'Goodnight.'

'Okay, 'night. See you in the morning.'

I reach over and find my Carl Jung book, sitting in the pile in the top corner of my bed. I slide my fingers down pages thirty-six and thirty-seven, where I marked a passage a few months ago. And then I find it—my favourite Jung quote, the one that inspired my current works.

The meeting of two personalities is like the contact of two chemical substances: if there is any reaction, both are transformed.

14

Two weeks fly by, and Annabelle is still sleeping on my couch. I'm enjoying having her here, but I'm also craving my own space, having my own place back. She plays her guitar most days, which I love, but then again . . . Yeah, it's a one-roomed house, and she's been here for six weeks now, and Johnny's arriving soon. Surely she's on her way to getting something sorted.

On Sunday morning, the day of Annabelle's interview with *Dazed & Confused*, we wake at the same time.

'You awake?' Annabelle calls out.

'Yeah, just reading.'

I roll over and look down at her. She's sitting on the couch with the rainbow-coloured crocheted rug wrapped around her shoulders. Her blonde hair is fuzzed up like Albert Einstein's, and her eyes are at half-squint. Her pink cherub lips stretch out into a grin, and I smile back at her.

We go out onto the verandah and sit together, rugged up, sipping coffee. Annabelle puts a ciggie between her lips and lights up. She inhales, then blows out a confident puff of smoke.

'Photographer from London,' she says. 'Remember? Tonight?'

My eyes wander all over the patchy lawn. 'I've been thinking about that, actually. You reckon he's gonna be single?'

Annabelle inhales again, and talks as she blows out. 'I know he is. As if he's going to have found a new girlfriend in a few weeks.'

'Well, some people move that quickly,' I say, wondering whether Annabelle will realise I'm referring to her.

'Well, not everyone's like me,' she says, making a strange facial expression which I read as *not everyone is as desirable as I am.*

'Are you still going into the city to meet with your manager?' I ask her.

'Shit,' Annabelle responds, spilling her coffee and rushing back inside. She calls back out to me, 'Thanks for reminding me, Joni. What would I do without you?'

I stay out on the verandah, enjoying the crisp, sunny morning. I conjure up a few images of what this photographer from London might look like. I see myself talking to him, kissing him, bringing him back to my place. But actually I can't see anything further happening, so my thoughts wander off into composing a talk I wanna have with Annabelle, asking her if she thinks she might be moving out soon.

When Annabelle is showered, she rushes back out onto the verandah. She's wearing a short pale-blue dress, her black fake-fur coat over the top, black boots, red lipstick and a bit of powder on her face. Her hair is razzed up, messy, tough and feminine. She smells like body wash and vanilla. All up, she looks like a superstar.

'See ya,' she says.

I watch her walk out the gate, and then I get straight into it. Dirty apron on over my PJs, fresh paints on my palette, clear water in my paint jars, and the final ingredient—my favourite song, 'Fade into You' by Mazzy Star.

Annabelle gave me *So Tonight That I Might See* when it first came out. I remember it was when I was living back at Mum and Dad's in The Cave, aka their garage. I immediately put the CD on and lay down on my bed. Listening to 'Fade into You' for the first time felt like the equivalent of putting a large chunk of Belgian milk chocolate in my mouth, and sucking on it. I felt as if I was floating on clouds up high, like the fluffy ones you look down on when you're in a plane. *Fade into you*—what a lyric! So romantic! Maybe I will fade into this hot, good-looking Londoner this evening.

I work on the painting of Annabelle and me for a few hours. Eventually my eyes need a break, so I walk out onto the verandah and stretch my arms to the sky, breathing deeply as a thin stream of low white cloud gently settles in.

'Hi Joni.'

It's Rebecca. Her hair is up in a brown-and-cream scarf, and she's holding secateurs in her garden-glove-covered hand. She's tending to the overgrown daisy bush that's beginning to take over the side of their back garden. How embarrassing! I'm still in my pyjamas! She puts the secateurs down, wipes her brow with her loose-fitting chambray shirt, and walks towards me. Her composure is calm and collected, centred and grounded.

'Cup of tea?' she asks, smiling. Her vowel sounds are rounded and warm.

'I'd love one,' I tell her.

'I'll put the kettle on,' she says, removing her gardening gloves.

'I'll just get changed,' I call out. I head back inside and take off my apron and pyjamas, then throw on an old red woollen dress, tidying up my hair as I walk back outside. I cross the lawn and wait patiently for her on her back deck, gazing down at my little bungalow. I take a good look, checking to see how easy it is for Rebecca and Peter to see through my kitchen window. The yard is quite large; the distance between the back of their house and my bungalow is at least twelve metres. But from what I can see, they're able to catch a glimpse of me if I forget to close the curtains on my kitchen window. I'm glad I'm pretty vigilant about keeping them closed. I walk around naked all the time, I sit at the kitchen table bawling my eyes out when I'm premenstrual, and sometimes I dance like a lunatic when I get home drunk.

Rebecca walks back out onto her deck carrying a wooden board on which she has placed some brie, crackers and sweet biscuits. We both sit down on the rouge-coloured lounge that faces the yard and my bungalow. I sit with my legs together, and feel myself taking on the persona of someone who is polite, reserved, less punk, less scatter-brained—all the things I think Rebecca is, in a nice way.

I wonder what we're going to talk about. I wait for her to initiate the conversation.

15

'I met your friend Annabelle a few days ago,' Rebecca tells me, once she's settled and sitting elegantly on the outdoor lounge. She slices a small section of brie with the fancy gold cheese-knife. 'We don't usually allow extra tenants.'

I'm suddenly struck with remorse, and my face becomes hot. I knew I should have checked with Rebecca and Peter. I knew it! I try to think of what to say, but before I can apologise, Rebecca kindly tells me: 'But with you, it's fine.'

I exhale, hoping she doesn't pick up on how worried I must look.

'Annabelle seems lovely. Are you two good friends?'

'Yeah, really good friends. Best friends,' I tell her, a little fearful that there may be something else I've done wrong. 'She won't be staying much longer. I'm so sorry.'

'Don't be, please. It really is okay. I've been enjoying hearing her singing and playing guitar. It's been making me . . . reminding me of when I was younger. I've been thinking about all my old housemates and . . . friends. I think that's why I asked you up for a cup of tea.' She lets out a small chuckle. 'To say thank you. It's lovely having you around. And Annabelle.'

The sound of the kettle whistling gradually becomes louder, and Rebecca excuses herself, walking back inside. I cut myself a huge slab of brie and place it on a cracker. The cheese is super creamy, and I know it would have cost a lot. Rebecca returns with a teapot, two cups, a sugar bowl and a milk jug— all sitting neatly on top of a doily on a silver tray. All the china is a new-looking version of what we have at Harland, except it's all matching and sparkling, and placed ever so symmetrically on the tray.

I wish I had Rebecca's composure. She is like a beautiful flower, whose roots are anchored firmly in the ground, and she has an inbuilt stillness, as though she's just returned from a Buddhist meditation retreat. Her speech is slow and precise; when I talk to her, her facial expressions show signs of empathy and compassion. She studies the way I wave my hands around when I describe things to her, quietly analysing my every move.

I guess this is what makes her suited to being a therapist. I wish she'd talk to me about her most complex patients, but I hear that therapists are not able to discuss their clients' issues. I've never been to see a psychologist, but Annabelle has, many times. She's told me all about it—what they say, what they do.

Rebecca pours me a cup of tea, her hands moving lightly between the cup and the teapot. 'Milk and sugar?' she asks quietly.

'Just milk, thanks.'

She hands me my milky tea.

'Peter's just written a play based on Harland,' she tells me. 'He's really happy with it, which is a plus.'

'Wow! I'd love to read it one day.'

Rebecca smiles, then sips.

'Did he meet Lucy? She owns Harland. She's French,' I tell her.

'Yes, we met Lucy a few months ago, when Peter was doing some research—needing to wander through the rooms. She's very beautiful.'

'I know,' I agree. 'She's an incredibly fiery woman. Did you pick up on that? She's moody, up and down, quite unpredictable. But then mesmerising, and . . . kind of like the Pied Piper, in a way. We're all really drawn to her. I love her sense of style.' I turn to Rebecca. 'I mean, you have great taste, and . . . you're really stylish too.'

Rebecca's personal style is very neat and plain, orderly and minimal. I often see her heading to work, and she always wears a crisp white shirt with a grey marle cashmere cardigan. And she'll wear a fine strand of pearls around her neck, with matching drop pearl earrings that hang from her perfect ear lobes. Her dark-brown hair is always blow-dried, and it falls neatly just above her shoulders. Her lips are full, and she wears a browny-red lipstick. Not too brown, not too red—the perfect blend. Sitting here right now, I feel myself bouncing back and forth between wishing I was like Lucy and then wishing I was like Rebecca, whose intellectual, precise and calm state is so unlike mine. I envy her deeply and, as our conversation develops, it's her I want to be, not Lucy.

'I remember she served us when we dined there, before Peter wandered around. She was very accommodating, but she did seem quite fiery. Actually, I saw her telling off one of the other waitresses. Very firm, her tone of voice.'

'Yeah, she's very moody. But I love her.'

Rebecca offers me another cup of tea. We both take a sip from our refilled cups, and she keeps the conversation running smoothly.

'I work with a lot of people who have mood disorders and complex obsessive tendencies, anger issues, et cetera. I'm very drawn to people like that.'

'I think I am too,' I tell Rebecca. 'A few weeks ago Lucy opened up to me about her childhood. Well . . . teenage years. And she had all these terrible operations, and complications when she had her period, and . . . I don't know whether I should go into detail, but she was very rebellious, and got up to all sorts of . . . silly things. I found it all so interesting, it was like I was watching a movie or something. I could have listened to her all night.'

'That's what my work is like,' Rebecca says, gracefully sipping her tea. 'I sit and listen to these incredibly personal tales. Interwoven private confessions, mistakes and regrets, pouring out all over me, from the minds of questioning, sensitive people who have lost their way. They're often caught up in their own self-constructed net. So many infidelities and insecurities. I'm enthralled by it all, but it's also quite draining.'

'It must be amazing. I like it when people offer up little pieces of their personal lives. I hate small talk,' I say, hoping she doesn't think I'm referring to what we're doing right now. Of course we're not, though, so why would she think that? I'm too paranoid. 'I'm only into having deep and meaningful relationships with people. I can't handle anything that's just chitchat.'

She picks up on my use of the word *relationship*, and asks me, 'Do you have a partner?'

'A boyfriend? No.'

'I only really started going out with men when I was in my early twenties,' she tells me. 'A similar age to you.'

She has the gift. The gift of making people feel like the way they live their life is normal. It's a gift, Annabelle tells me, that all good therapists possess. And then Rebecca opens up her glory box and gives me more of what I adore.

'I had a girlfriend when I was eighteen. I don't tell many people about that, but you're an art student, or . . . sorry—you're an artist, so you're in with the world of women on women, men on men.' She gives me a warm smile.

'What was that like?' I ask.

'Complex, beautiful, heartbreaking. I thought we'd be together forever, but then she ended it. It was like a Shakespeare tragedy, really.' Rebecca laughs. 'But I'm a grown woman now. Peter and I have been married for almost ten years. We're still very much in love. He's so good to me. I know it's a classic cliché, but he really is my soul mate.'

'I can see that,' I tell her.

'We're growing old together. Both in our forties now.' She smiles, reaching for a cracker.

'Oh. You look so young,' I tell her, holding tight to my teacup.

'Aww, that's sweet of you, although I love getting older. I've always had an old soul. People used to tell me that when I was a child. I feel more myself now I'm in my forties. Don't ever let anyone tell you that getting older is depressing! Your forties are a great decade. You don't worry so much about how you look, and you begin to realise how much knowledge and wisdom you've gained over the years. You know how to look after yourself, what you want, what you need.'

She's the polar opposite of Lucy. Rebecca—a classic

beauty with an old soul, moving gracefully into middle age, poised, with a tranquil disposition. Lucy—young at heart (or clinging desperately to her youth, depending on what way you want to look at it), drunkenly dancing on a tabletop with a ciggie hanging out of her mouth, cleavage, short skirt, grabbing someone's bum.

Ha ha! I laugh on the inside, and realise I'm able to appreciate the beauty in both of these older women. I'm like neither, but they both possess qualities that I admire. I wonder what life will be like for me when I'm that age.

Rebecca puts her teacup down on the little outdoor coffee table.

'It's my forty-sixth birthday in a few weeks,' she tells me.

'Got any party plans?' I ask her.

'Oh, I don't really have parties anymore. Peter and I will probably go out for dinner. Perhaps see a play.' She chuckles with a lovely rounded tone. 'My nieces are coming over for cake on the actual day, which will be nice.'

Rebecca reaches over for a cracker and picks up the cheese knife. 'As you know, Peter and I don't have children. We decided early on that we didn't want any. Peter's such an introvert, and I've never cared much for having a baby. I wanted a career.'

'Mum tells me I can have both.' I immediately regret having said this. I don't want to offend her, or start any type of argument.

Before I can correct myself, she says in a smooth tone, 'I know, I know. A lot of women juggle both beautifully. I just use that as a simple excuse to explain why having children is not right for me, because I don't think many people understand that some women actually don't want them in their lives. They think there's something wrong with us.'

'Oh, I completely respect you.'

'Thanks, Joni.' She raises her teacup, giving me an English-country-garden cheers.

I place my cup back on the tray, and explain to her that I need to get back to work in my studio space as I'm keen to finish the painting I'm working on. She tells me she understands the work ethic of a creative—Peter is the same. If a day goes by when he hasn't had the chance to make any progress on the play he's working on, he'll be in a rotten mood and unbearable to live with. We both stand, and Rebecca slips her fingers back into her gardening gloves.

'Bye, and thank you for the tea and cheese.'

'My pleasure,' she says, getting back into trimming the daisy bush.

I walk down the stairs and across the lawn, hoping that one day I'll meet someone who feels like my soul mate. Someone who adores me as much as I adore them. Someone I connect with emotionally. Someone who loves me for who I am.

Wandering through the front door of my bungalow, I feel embarrassed by the mess, comparing myself to Rebecca's neat orderliness. But my urge to paint is far greater than my urge to tidy up, so I throw my apron back on and head over to the canvas.

And then—damn!—the phone starts ringing.

'Hello?'

'Joni, oh Joni!'

It's Annabelle, sobbing uncontrollably. She is an absolute mess.

'Annabelle, what is it? Take a deep breath. What's happened?'

'Johnny's not coming! He's not coming, Joni!'

'Well, maybe you can fly over there to be with him. You've always told me you love New York.' I try to offer her a positive slant on the news that has left her so devastated.

'He . . .' she howls, her voice distorted. She sniffs an unimaginable amount of snot up her nose, and makes a few awful animal-like yowling sounds. 'He's seeing someone else.'

I knew this was going to happen. I knew it! But weirdly, comforting her does gives me strength. I'd forgotten about this feeling. She's fallen to her knees, and she needs me.

'Look, Annabelle, where are you?'

'I'm in the city.'

'Where in the city?'

'In a—awww—phone box,' she cries.

'Okay, calm down, you will get through this. Slow down your breathing. It's all right, I'm here for you.'

She goes off on a longwinded, tangled-up explanation of why she thinks this has happened, how she can't believe she fell for him, how she doesn't think she's going to cope with doing the photos and interview tonight. I hardly understand any of it, because it's all broken up with huge sniffs and the sound of her wiping her hand over her face and mouth, mopping up her tears.

'Cancel the photos. Cancel the interview,' I suggest, taking a pragmatic approach.

'No! Are you crazy? This interview could break me in the UK.'

You're already broken. But I know what she means. She really cares about her music; she wants to make it on an international level, and I feel confident that she will.

'Okay, yep, we want this interview to go ahead. I think you need to come back to my house now, and hang out here for a while. You can have a shower, I'll make you some food, you can relax. We'll deal with this together.'

'Okay, okay,' she says.

It's one of the many great things about Annabelle. She does usually listen to me and take my orders during times like this. I think the last three times she's been in this state, she's come straight to me, and I've helped her calm down, get it together, look at the big picture. And I enjoy taking on this role. The role of the nurturer. It makes me feel better when I try to make Annabelle feel better.

We say goodbye to each other, and she tells me she'll jump on the next bus back to my place. I promptly take my apron off and hang it on the hook on the wall.

16

Mushroom risotto always tastes better with real butter. I check the fridge. Yep, got some. Before I start cooking, I put a record on. John Coltrane—*Blue Train*. Dad got me onto it. He always has it playing in his bookshop. It's calming, fluid, a little sultry. Perfect for standing over the stovetop while I slowly stir nonstop for twenty minutes.

When the arborio rice is cooked right through, I turn off the hot plate and cover the risotto with the saucepan lid. I do a quick tidy-up, light some incense, turn the record over, put my apron back on and continue to work away on my painting. I lose myself in the lines, the curves, the composition, the colours, and then realise that the second side of the record finished ages ago. Weird. I thought Annabelle would be here by now.

I imagine her—crying, tear-wiping—on the bus as it weaves in and out of traffic, grinding to a halt at every stop. And then she'd press the button—*ding!*—and stand up, holding on to the poles, wobbling her way towards the back door.

Over an hour passes, and when I look up and check the clock I see that it's time for me to get ready for work. Where is Annabelle? I hope she's okay. I rinse my brushes with turps in the bathroom sink. It always stinks the house out, so I keep the bathroom door closed and the fan on.

The sound of the water splashing into the sink collides with the rattle of the fan—it's a thin chugalug of mechanical white noise mixed with a heavy downpour on a tin roof. My hands are stained with paint—purple-blue fingers and palms. I scrub them extra hard, splashing turps all over them, rinsing them until they're almost back to their beige-pink selves. Then I write a note, and leave it on the kitchen bench.

> *Annabelle,*
>
> *How are you? I cooked a mushroom risotto for you (it's on the stove), although you've probably eaten lunch by now. Help yourself to anything. Take a hot shower, rest up. I'll see you at Harland tonight. (Exciting!!!)*
>
> *Love Joni xxx*
>
> *PS: You are totally amazing and you're the most beautiful person I know. Johnny doesn't deserve you. You're the best! I love you. Call me at Harland if you need to: 815 4286 xxxxxxx*

As I'm getting dressed for work, I think again about the possibility of the photographer from London being extremely good-looking. I can't deny it, I'm hoping something does happen between me and him. *Wear something good, wear something sexy,* I say to myself, baffled by my choice of words. *Wear something sexy?* Who do I think I am?

Six of my dresses end up inside out, one on top of the other, on my floor. And then I become so rushed and nervous that I can't think straight—I can't put an outfit together. And then I enter dud world, and I can tell my neck and cheeks are red. Flustered. Ridiculously flustered, that's what I am, and now I feel as though I can't possibly wear anything that will draw attention to myself.

Why do I always do this? It's my nervous gene. I got it from Mum—she'd always act as calm as, but then, whenever they had an opening at the gallery, she'd start talking quickly and dropping things. She'd get a red face, and I could smell her BO. I know that sounds terrible—Mum's nervous BO. Awww, what a gem. I love Mum.

I end up walking out the door in my shabby, plain black dress—the one I bought at Balmain Market for five dollars. And then outside, away from the heater, I realise I need a second layer on, so I unlock the front door, walk back inside and grab my cropped brown woollen jumper. I catch myself in the mirror: plain and boring. My hair is out, a little knotty, and my brown Blundstone boots on my small feet await their scolding from Lucy. *Please can you wear some shoes that are a little more dressy, Joni?*

Once I'm out the side gate, riding down the centre of my street, I squint. Partly due to the cold, early evening breeze, and partly because I can't stop wondering where Annabelle is. She's obviously decided to go somewhere else, or do something else. But where, and what?

The *cling* and *clang* of a car towing a rusty empty trailer down Darling Street startles me, and I swerve closer to the left-hand side of the road, gripping the handlebars tight. I pedal past the Emerald. It looks full, bubbling, with the usual Sunday evening get-togethers.

Further down on Darling Street I pick up speed, shivering as the icy air blows right through my woollen jumper and smashes straight into my skin. Bloody hell! I should have worn a jacket. As I huff and puff up the hill, I look into the windows of the small houses and cottages. It's that time of day when everyone has their lights on, but has not yet closed the curtains—my favourite time. I imagine the insides of all the rooms as miniatures in a museum. Dioramas. Little handmade doll's houses with tiny people and replica furniture.

Then I stand up on my pedals, pushing hard, bum up off the seat, continuing to take on the hill. My hair flies in the wintry breeze, kissing my cheeks, each strand behaving like a wind sock. I hope this interview goes okay tonight. Annabelle was so beside herself when she found out her favourite UK fashion and music mag wanted to do a story on her. It's just nuts! I can't imagine that ever happening to me with my career as an artist. I want to exhibit overseas, but I feel like I have such a long way to go.

I pull up in front of Harland.

'Joni, hi.'

It's Michael, arriving at the same time as me. He's had his dark-brown hair cut—a little shorter around the sides, still long on top. His three-day growth is more obvious than usual, his eyes are tired-looking. He acts as though he's apologising for saying hello, as though I may not recognise him. I can tell he's the kind of guy that would tolerate anything, and not speak up for himself, ever. As though he'd avoid every conflict thrown at him. This is his usual disposition—he puts everyone in front of himself at all times. And he's sort of sorry. Sorry for everything— for arriving at the same time as me, for not really knowing what to say. He makes me feel much more entitled and special than I really am.

He opens the side gate and gestures for me to go in before him. The tyres on my bike roll up the slight step at the start of the side path. Michael follows. I don't look back, but I can tell he would have closed the gate very gently, put his hands in his pockets and transitioned into his usual shuffle, while trying to draw the least amount of attention to himself. He's below me in class and status, and he put himself there. I don't even know anything about his upbringing or education, and I don't think I've told him much about mine. He's probably overheard me talking to the others; but either way, for some reason he places himself on a lower rank. On the bottom shelf. He does it to everyone at Harland, even Simon. He's comfortable there, on that lower level, I think.

'How was your day?' I ask him, turning, still wheeling my bike down the side path.

'Oh, you know . . . pretty good,' he answers, avoiding eye contact.

We leave it at that and I lean my bike against the shed, hanging my helmet over the handlebars. Dave bounces down the back stairs holding a large stainless-steel bowl, beating something up with a whisk. He has his white chef hat on, which always makes me laugh. It's too pro for him. Too clichéd. He looks like he's in costume for a dress-up party. He gives me a quick, 'Hey Joni,' and takes Michael inside, talking nonstop about butter and pastry and pie dishes.

Before following them up the stairs, I turn towards the garden. The ivy, lying low, splays out with its beautiful jagged leaves—pointy, triangular and organically symmetrical, each with their own imperfections. I walk closer to the garden bed so I can smell the earth. It's damp, dark, bottle-green. Lucy must have watered it when she arrived this evening. Tiger-Lily catches my eye, gracefully walking along the boards of the verandah.

I skip up the stairs and open the back door. It's warm, golden, sumptuous, old-worldly; it's even more gorgeous in here than it was last night. All of my senses are filled right up to the brim. I'm so glad I work here.

'Joni darling!' Lucy greets me with a kiss-kiss on each cheek. It's lovely being loved by Lucy. I hope she doesn't slip into the other side, and lash out at me at some point during the evening.

'Can you get started on setting Gatsby—two twos. I've got the Red Room set up for Annabelle, and Lillibon is done. Juliet's down setting up the Pines. Oh, and can you get the fires going?'

'Okay.'

'Thanks, my love.'

No time for a pre-dinner coffee/catch-up with Dave tonight. I drop my backpack in the corner near the hatstand and get straight into it.

'Coffee, Joni?' Lucy calls out.

'Oh my god, that would be amazing. Thanks, Lucy!' I call back, pulling cutlery out from the velvet-lined drawer in the hallway sideboard.

Lucy brings my coffee into Gatsby and then I sip as I go, quickly getting the tables in order. When the table below the window is done, I swiftly move on to setting the other table for two. The old-fashioned crystal wine glasses are placed to the top right of the tarnished, worn silver cutlery. A green cut-glass vase, holding a single pink rose, is positioned in the centre of each table. *There!* Both tables look beautiful.

I head back out through the Bar Room and down to the shed, where I grab a handful of firewood. I stack it up, log upon log, attempting to hug it in towards my body, carrying it like a woman in the woods in a fairytale, just how Lucy does it every night. As I struggle back up the stairs, several logs topple out of my arms, falling from my poorly-put-together pile. I feel a splinter dig into my right hand, and then I kick my boot into the top step, tripping and turning, then dropping the entire bundle as I fall down onto the back verandah.

Shit! At this point Lucy, startled by the deadened boom and bang of the tumbling firewood, opens the back door. I'm on my hands and knees like a dog, with the unfortunate added bonus that my bum is now facing Lucy. I know she can see my undies.

'Joni?'

My knees are scratched and cut, and my hands hurt. I feel like a little kid.

'Joni,' Lucy repeats. 'This is James, and he's here for the interview.'

What? The photographer from London?

'Hi there,' says a deep voice.

I look towards denim-clad legs, too embarrassed to look up any further. Then—hang on a minute—I realise his accent is completely Aussie. He must be an assistant or something. Argh. I guess I should get up.

'Joni, could you show him into the Red Room, please. I'll take care of lighting the fires,' Lucy says, clutching on to her new-found affection for me while desperately trying to suppress the undertones of disappointment and scorn.

I pick myself up and dust my knees off. My finger-tips are bloody. My right knee is grazed. I wipe my hands on my black dress and follow Lucy and the guy back into the Bar Room. I push past Lucy, past the guy—James, or whatever—and confidently stride along the hallway towards the Red Room.

'This way,' I tell him, not bothering to bring a menu in or anything. I'll just chuck him in there to wait for the others.

'Thanks,' he says. 'I'll start bringing the gear in.'

I quickly wash my hands in the basin of the outhouse toilet, then I head back into the Bar Room, hoping that Dave might bring some dinner out to us soon. To my delight, it's already on the table. Five rosy bowls filled with creamy pasta, a sugar bowl filled with freshly cut parsley, an enamel mug filled with grated parmesan cheese, salt, pepper, and a fresh baguette lying next to a slab of butter. Yum! I get stuck into it. Michael sits with me, and we smile at each other as we eat the rich, heavy meal.

When we're close to finishing, I'm cut short by the tinkle of the bells on the front door—a sound we don't often hear before six.

'Ah, Lucy!' says a girly voice. Then *bang-bang, shuffle, clip-clop* and a slurred 'Is Joni here?'

I turn my head towards the hallway, and a drunken (more accurately, *sloshed*) Annabelle stumbles into the Bar Room. 'Joooniii!'

She's embarrassingly blind. I sit her down, and break her off a decent-sized piece of baguette.

'Eat!' I order her.

I don't want to hear about it. Where she's been, how much she's drunk. I place a jug of water and a glass in front of her, move over to the coffee machine, and begin to make her a double-shot latte.

I lean my head back towards her, as the hot water runs through the coffee grounds. 'We need to sort you out. This interview is gonna be good for you. We want it to go well.'

She eats the baguette, slumping over the table as if to say *I've given up on life, but I'm so drunk now that it sort of feels like everything is okay.* She looks at me, slowly becoming aware of her inebriated state, but completely unaware of her liquor stench.

'I was wondering where you were,' I tell her sternly.

Michael sits watching and listening. Annabelle's tail curls up between her legs. She's sorry, I know it. But I need to help her sort herself out. Sober up.

I turn towards the kitchen. 'Dave, have you got any more . . .'

'Yep, bringing some out now.'

He brings out another serving of the creamy pasta and places it in front of Annabelle. He's so intuitive. He knows what's going on. He always saves the day.

'Sorry, Joni . . . it was just such . . . I can't believe that Johnny . . . I've just been in the city . . .'

'Just eat,' I tell her firmly.

Juliet and Simon walk through the back door together and sit straight down, tucking into their pasta.

'I got a lot of work done today,' Juliet slurps, her mouth full.

'Good on you,' Michael responds.

'Six resin bangles done, and set and polished. I'm on fire!' Juliet drips creamy sauce on her already stained bright-green cardigan. Her hair is up in two oversized Princess Leia bread-roll buns, and her ludicrously loud Minnie Mouse earrings *donk* against her neck, as she toggles her head from side to side.

'Annabelle, this is Juliet. Juliet—Annabelle,' I say, gesturing.

'Hey,' Annabelle slurs.

'We met in January,' Juliet blurts.

Annabelle pretends to remember. 'Oh yeah.'

'And Michael, Simon—Annabelle. My best friend, who needs sobering up before her interview.'

'Joni, I'm just tipsy. I'm not drunk.'

'I think I've seen you in the paper,' Simon says, croaky-voiced.

'Yeah, she's an incredible singer. And songwriter,' I tell him.

'Oh yeah,' Michael adds. 'I've seen you play. You were amazing!'

Mmm, Simon and Michael come to life in Annabelle's presence. Typical.

I leave them to chat, and go check on Aussie James in the Red Room. I walk along the hallway, and see him lugging lights and metal stands through the front door. I catch a glimpse of his face. Gosh, I didn't notice before. He's . . . unusually cute.

17

'Do you need a hand?' I ask politely.

'I'm right, thanks,' James answers, smiling. 'You okay after that fall out there?'

'Oh yeah, that was . . . embarrassing. Sorry about that.'

He carries two metal stands into the Red Room, and I can't help but follow him in.

'This room's gorgeous,' he says, admiring the urns and vases, then turns towards all the Valentine's Day cards surrounding the door.

'I know. It was my idea.' I immediately regret trying to take credit for suggesting the Red Room as the perfect spot for the interview and shoot.

'Well, you have a good eye,' he says, looking directly at me. He has beautiful eyes. Dark brown. And they're sad. He has sad eyes. Sad, but kind of playful at the same time, with an underlying *I don't follow the crowd, I climb fences at night, on my own, and I take photos of abandoned factories and infinite fields beside winding roads.* I feel like I know him, yet I don't. Like I can read him, but I can't. He's . . . mysterious, yet familiar.

I can't move.

I try to act casual. 'I . . . are . . . I mean, are you the assistant to the photographer from London?'

'Oh no,' James answers, running his hands over one of the stands, then undoing its black screw slowly. 'He wasn't able to make it.'

His voice is mellow, warm, low. He's tall, lanky—although *lanky* is too ugly a word to describe him. The strands of his shoulder-length, layered brown hair fall softly around his olive-skinned face. He looks European, perhaps, and his mouth is a tiny bit crooked; but that doesn't let his overall handsomeness down. Not to me, anyway. I smooth my black dress down with my sweaty hands. Is it too short? I wish I'd worn something else tonight.

'So . . . *you're* the photographer?'

As soon as I say it, I'm paranoid that it sounded as though I think he's just the consolation prize. That he's amateur photo boy—nowhere near as good as the London professional.

'Yeah. I used to shoot for *Dazed & Confused* when I lived in London. Last year.'

'Oh.' I look at the black buttons on his brown woollen knee-length coat. He wears it open, with a knitted black jumper underneath. Black jeans. Blundstone boots. Like mine. A muddled-up thought pattern is taking shape inside my head. I want to be him. And I want him. All to myself. It's a cocktail of attraction and admiration—shaken, not stirred. James smiles at me, and I almost can't take it. The immediacy of this sensation is making me feel strange and . . . sort of frightened, because I have no control over it.

'I've worked with Polly quite a bit,' he tells me, pulling his camera out of its case. His hands are gently masculine.

'Who's Polly?'

'Polly . . . lovely Polly.' He places his camera on the table. 'She's going to be interviewing Annabelle. She's an incredible journalist. Very funny. You'll love her.'

I dip down, as though I'm on a rollercoaster and falling from the top. Who is this Polly? Are she and James an item? Where does James live now? What does he love? What does he hate? What's his favourite food? I want to climb into his world.

He smiles at me as though he can hear my thoughts, and I'm bowled over by his adorable mouth. His full lips. His unconventional face. He has such an offbeat beauty.

'Okay then, I should . . . get back into . . .' I awkwardly point towards the hallway, 'the Bar Room . . . I've got some setting up to do. Can I get you anything?'

'Oh, I'm fine. I'll just be setting up.' He gives a little laugh, and I know it's because we both just said *setting up*. 'We're gonna do the shoot first. Is Annabelle far away?'

'Ah, she's out . . . out in the Bar Room. You want me to bring her in?'

'No rush. It's going to take me a while to get things set up in here. I'll come and get her when I'm ready.'

'Okay,' I tell him, in the most attractive vocal tone I can produce.

I walk back along the hallway. *Holy-God-Jesus-Mother . . .*

'Joni, is Gatsby set?' Lucy almost bumps into me as she hurriedly sets up champagne glasses on a tray.

'Um . . .' I can't even think. *Focus Joni, focus.* I try to snap out of my James fixation, but it's all James, James, James.

'Yep, it's set,' I tell Lucy, pretending I've got it together.

'Great!'

I sit back down at the staff table, and finish off the last of my dinner while in a daze.

'Incredible pasta, Dave!' Annabelle shouts out, and I can tell she's still drunk.

'Thanks, Annabelle!' Dave calls back from the kitchen. He pokes his head through the doorway into the Bar Room. 'Joni told me all about Johnny Harrison! That's so amazing! I know his music.'

I turn, and rush towards Dave. Then, while making sure Annabelle can't see my face, I do the slitting-throat gesture, clenching my jaw, baring my teeth. Dave shuts up, looking confused. I glance down the hallway, still doing the clenched-jaw/slitting-throat thing, and there's James, watching me. I quickly try to shift into relaxed, easygoing, pretty face; but it's too late, he's seen me at my ugliest. Why did I do that stupid throat slit?

James smiles, and it's a warm, *you're funny* smile. I think he might . . . only might, and I may be wrong . . . but I think there's the *tiniest bit of a possibility* that he might like me. Just a bit. Maybe. But I'm sure he has a girlfriend. Guys like that aren't single.

I walk back to my spot at the staff table and catch Lucy flicking through the bookings diary. She turns sharply towards Juliet. 'Love, you can take care of the Pines tonight. They are regulars, and they like their champagne and tight service. I need you to keep the standard high.'

Juliet chews on a torn-off piece of baguette, looking out at Tiger-Lily seducing the window.

'Juliet!' Lucy snaps.

'Yep, got it. I saw them in the book. I served them last time. It's all good.'

'And Joni, we can both take care of Gatsby, but you do Lillibon, and I'll handle the Red Room.'

Damn. Why has she given me Lillibon? I want the Red Room.

'I'm happy to do the Red Room,' I suggest, in the hope that Lucy will capriciously change her mind and give it to me.

'I've got it, my love. I'll take care of them.'

Lucy seductively tosses her head, so that the ends of her wavy blonde locks fall gently on her breasts. She's got her tight, blood-red velvet dress on, the one with the low cleavage. A fine line of black liquid eyeliner on her lids, rosy rouge on her cheeks, gold hoop earrings. She looks incredible, like a movie star on her way to the Oscars in the mid-1960s. I know James is gonna fall for her. I just know it. My chances are over. James and Joni. Gone.

'Hi darling!' A super-cute, bubbly female voice spills into the Bar Room from the hallway. The accent is distinctly English.

'Polly!'

I peek around the doorway and spy James greeting a woman with a kiss-kiss on either cheek. Lucy slides past me and walks on through.

'Hi, I'm Polly, for the interview with Annabelle Reed.'

'Lovely to meet you. I'm Lucy.'

I notice Lucy hamming up her French accent.

'Oh, you're French,' Polly bubbles, the inflection in her voice bouncing all over the place.

'*Oui.*'

'Love Paris. Absolutely love it.'

Polly sounds fun. I walk up to say hi.

'I'm Joni,' I shake her hand, then feel awkward and businesslike. *Wrong greeting, Joni. Wrong greeting.* 'Annabelle's just out the back,' I tell her. 'Should I . . .'

'Can I get you two a drink?' Lucy cuts in, moving over to block me from Polly.

Okay, I get the picture. I'm not needed here. Lucy's taking over.

'Oh, I'd love a champers,' Polly puffs out, casually removing her long mustard-coloured cardigan. Her turquoise skirt and red stockings kind of clash with her stripey pink-and-blue jumper, but in a good way. She's like a mismatched, happy-colour bomb. Her teeth are slightly bucked, and her eyes have laugh wrinkles in the corners. Probably in her late twenties, maybe thirty. She spells out *thrown-together, fun-loving British gal.* And she looks like she loves a good party. Lots of Pimm's and lemonade, and dancing until dawn. That's what they drink, Annabelle told me.

I walk back towards the Bar Room, overhearing Polly's effervescent questioning. 'How long you been back, James? We miss you!'

'Nearly six months.'

'Really!' Polly cries out, in gobsmacked falsetto. She lowers her tone, adding, 'It's hot in London now. Well, London hot. I'm so glad you were available, James. Bloody Robin, bailing on me.'

I return to the staff table as Juliet gets up—pen and pad in hand—and rushes off down to the Pines. Dave turns the kitchen radio off, as per Lucy's instruction, and the woozy strings on the first track of the Josephine Baker CD fill the restaurant. Annabelle chats to Michael, and he listens and nods and yeps and agrees with everything she's saying.

'Michael, I need you in here, mate!' Dave calls out.

'Coming.'

Annabelle slouches and delivers a deep sigh. 'They're here, aren't they,' she says, sounding as though she wishes the whole thing had been called off.

'Yes,' I tell her. 'And the photographer is a total babe!'

'I told you,' Annabelle says. She reaches into her handbag, pulls out a hand mirror and applies a fresh coat of red lipstick. Then out comes her powder compact. As she starts dabbing the powder puff all over her face, I give her the finer details.

'It's not the London guy. He's not coming. He's Australian. The photographer. Annabelle, I'm . . . I'm really attracted to him. Like, I'm talking *really* attracted to him.'

Annabelle doesn't respond, and I know it's because she got dumped today. *Internationally, over-the-phone, humiliatingly and already replaced* dumped. She pulls a cigarette out of her bag and lights up.

'You're supposed to have that out the back once the restaurant's open,' I tell her, ushering her out the door.

'It's freezing out here!' she cries from the back verandah, trying to force me to let her back inside.

'Rug on the chair,' I tell her, pointing to the red-and-black mohair rug Lucy wraps herself in while on her ciggie breaks.

I put my apron on and check the bookings diary. My Lillibon booking should be here soon. I tidy the bench and faff around a little, peeking out through the hallway for another glimpse of James.

Annabelle comes back inside, reeking of cigarette smoke. She pulls out a bottle of vanilla perfume from her bag, and sprays her neck. Smoke and sweets, her signature combo. 'I'd better get in there,' she says. 'Do I look okay?'

I do a quick once-over of her face, ruffle her hair up a little, and straighten her black faux fur coat.

'You look great,' I tell her reassuringly. 'Go get 'em!'

I give her a warm smile, and she embraces me lovingly.

'Thanks, Joni. I mean it.'

'It's what I'm here for.'

I watch her walk up the step and into the hallway. Then five seconds later:

'Annabelle, my god, you look gorgeous!' It's Polly, over the top and cheerily starstruck. 'Everyone is *loving* your new single with Johnny Harrison. We've heard it. Got an advance copy.'

'Yeah, thanks,' I hear Annabelle say in her cool, confident rock-star voice. I feel relieved, sensing that she's easily been able to switch from depressive drunk to professional singer-songwriter.

Polly continues, 'Oh Annabelle—James. James—Annabelle.'

The sound of his name is enough to set my heart racing. I try to listen in to more of their conversation, then get disrupted by Lucy's 'Joni, your group for Lillibon are here.'

'Okay, cool.'

I walk along the hallway to greet them with a quick 'Hello, come this way,' while trying to catch a glimpse of James in the Red Room. I manage to, only for a speck of a second, but it's enough to give me a small frisson.

I seat my group of eight in Lillibon, sliding my body between the chairs and the ivy wallpaper, placing napkins on their laps.

They seem a conservative lot—a group of older women, all with short, dyed, styled hair. A few fob chains, a mix of strong floral perfumes, polite conversation, friendly compliments. I feel comfortable in their presence.

I fiddle around in the drawer of the sideboard in the hall, digging out my notepad and pen. Slipping both into the pocket of my apron, I head towards the front door. As I pass the Red Room I pretend that I'm checking on something, even though there's no need whatsoever for me to be there. I turn the doorhandle and peer out onto the street, pretending that I'm looking for someone.

And there goes Annabelle's voice. It stands out above everyone else's, and it hurts. Hurts me deep inside.

'James, I love your coat. Do you know Andrew Webb? Brilliant Australian photographer . . . You do? Would you teach me how to take photos? I'm hopeless. Take me into your darkroom? Ooh la la, James, that would be lovely, you and me in a dark room together . . . We should hang out after the interview. Will you? I'd love to play you some of my new songs.'

She's flirting with him! I can't believe it. It's as if she's transformed into a completely different person. I walk past the Red Room and give her a dirty look. She mouths back: 'What?'

Lucy passes me on her way into the room, her gold bracelets tinkling. She places her hand on James's shoulder, handing him a beer. Everyone's on James. Everyone.

I glance into Gatsby, continuing with the *pretending I'm busy* act. When I turn for one more look at James in the Red Room, I catch him taking the lens cap off his camera. All the women in the room have their eyes on him. He looks up through the doorway at me, and gives me a wink. I die. I walk through to Lillibon, feeling light-headed.

I'm going to tell Dave. After I take the drink orders, I'm telling Dave.

18

My ladies in Lillibon are beginning to lighten up. One of them is giving a drawn-out history of cuckoo clocks as the others stare inquisitively at the example hanging on the wall. When the history lesson is over, I take their drink orders, which are a mix of sparkling water and wine.

When I dash back into the Bar Room, I poke my head into the kitchen. 'Dave,' I half-talk, half-whisper, beckoning for him to come closer.

He flips a tea towel over his shoulder and wipes the sweat off his brow with his forearm. 'What is it?'

'The photographer,' I hiss, feeling my whole face come to life.

'What? Guy from London?'

'No. He's Australian.'

'What? Hang on. I thought the . . .'

'Guy from London couldn't make it. But James . . . oh my god. He's the replacement.' I edge in even closer and whisper in his ear. 'Dave, he's so cute!'

Dave does his hilarious eyebrows-raised, not-showing-teeth, silly smile. He drops his tea towel on the bench and, with one hand swipe, neatens up his hair. He ventures along the hallway as I try to call him back, but it's too late.

He reaches the Red Room and stands in the doorway, observing. I stare into his eyes as he walks back towards me.

'Annabelle's all over him,' he announces.

'Yeah, but . . . he just winked at me, and I kind of think there might be something between us.'

'Well, get rid of that idea, babe, because Annabelle is in there, and she's reeling him in. I told you she . . .' He glances into the kitchen. 'Shit! The bacon!'

As I'm preparing the drinks for Lillibon, Dave pokes his head into the Bar Room. 'We'll talk more about this later.' He disappears for a moment and then leans into the Bar Room again. 'My advice is—if you want him, you've got to go in there and show Annabelle who's boss.' He glances back at the bacon frying in the pan, then asks, 'Is he single?'

'God, who knows?'

'Okay,' Dave advises. 'Assume he is, and go in there and Joni it up for him. Got it?'

'Yes, Dave. I've got it. Don't worry. I'm onto it.'

I find the chablis, pour two glasses and set them up on a tray. Lucy is elegantly walking towards the back door, directing the large group who are to be seated down in the Pines. They all look tall, sophisticated, businessy.

Suddenly Juliet bursts through the back door, almost knocking Lucy over. 'Sorry, darling,' Juliet apologises to Lucy and then, in a girl-guides-leader voice, tells the group: 'Follow me!'

Lucy and I roll our eyes at each other. Bloody Juliet. I pour the last of the tumblers of sparkling water for the Lillibon ladies, and notice Lucy hanging around close by, moving cups this way and that on top of the coffee machine.

'James is pretty cute,' she comments.

'Yeah, he's okay,' I reply, as though I've hardly noticed him.

'You look a bit like you might have the hots for him,' she continues.

'What? No I don't. You do.'

'Me? Joni, I'm taken.'

'But you were flirting with him.'

'No, I wasn't. I was just being friendly. Welcoming. It's my restaurant. I want people to feel at home.'

'You literally hugged him when you gave him his beer.' I regret going this far. Why am I being like this? Why don't I just be honest? 'Sorry . . . I . . .'

'Joni. He's your kind of guy. Not mine. I've got Dave, darling. Plus I saw the way he was looking at you.' She comes in closer. 'You do have the hots for him, don't you?' she teases.

I smile, with my lips closed.

'I can read you, Joni. Go on, admit it. You have!'

Lucy grabs herself a port glass, and pulls the cork out of a port bottle. She pours herself her favourite beverage, and swings over to the staff table, sitting on top, crossing her legs. She takes a sip.

'You do, you so do. You've got the hots for him, I can see it,' she says, with a cheeky semi-smile.

'Okay,' I confess. 'Yes, yes, okay. I have . . . I do . . . think he's my kind of guy. The kind of guy I go for.' I can't look her in the face. I'm too embarrassed.

'*Je te l'avais dit!*'

'Huh?'

Lucy dramatically snaps her fingers, up high in front of her, gold bangles jingling. 'I knew it!' she cries. 'I know you, Joni Johnson. Better than you think.'

She grabs another port glass and fills it, hands it to me, and offers me a cheers. We clink glasses, and she announces, 'And you, my love, are going home with him tonight.'

'Aaah!' I shriek, before sipping the sweet, syrupy wine.

'That's the plan, my lady,' she tells me.

'But Annabelle's . . .'

'I can see what she's doing. Don't worry. We're switching.'

'What?'

'I'm going Lillibon, you're going Red Room.'

'Really?'

'Really.' Lucy drinks the remainder of her port. 'And we'll still share Gatsby. There are two tables coming in soon. What's this?' She gestures towards the tray of drinks I've put together for the group in Lillibon.

'Let me deliver it, and then we change over, yeah?' I suggest.

'Good plan, Joni. I've taught you well.'

Of course she takes credit for my simple suggestion—but tonight I'm not judging her behaviour. She is on my side! She is on my side!

I deliver the tray of drinks hurriedly, worried that my breath stinks of port. The women's voices are rounded, and they sound like dear, close friends—probably all known each other since childhood. I leave them be and draw a deep, excited breath.

I flick my hair back, the way I've seen Lucy do, and I hold my head up high. I wander into the Red Room, and check James and Polly's glasses.

Polly's—empty. Then James—his beer glass is two-thirds empty. And then my eyes shift from his beer glass up over his jeans, all around his torso, through his chest, and up to his face. His features are so unconventional. But he's extremely good-looking. He has his tripod facing the red velvet curtains, and is loading film into the back of his camera.

'Oh, that's going to be gorgeous, James!' Polly exclaims. 'Hop in, Annabelle darling.'

Annabelle—almost on top of James, watching him load the film—is oblivious to Polly's request.

'Why don't you go over and stand in front of the curtains, Annabelle,' James suggests. I may be wrong, but his body language suggests that he's not really that into her overly flirtatious behaviour.

'Can I get you another beer, James?' I ask, trying to sound professional.

'Oooh, I'd love a top-up,' Polly pipes, before James can respond.

'Ah, yeah,' James answers, concentrating on attaching his camera to his tripod. Then he looks at me, and says, 'Thanks.'

I melt. 'Two more drinks coming up.'

'What about me?' Annabelle whines.

'Oh. What would you like, Annabelle?' I ask her, hoping she picks up on my disappointment with the way she's flirting with James, and my disapproval with her ordering *more* alcohol.

'Gin and tonic, thanks, Joni.'

She's talking down to me. Even after we hugged and loved in the Bar Room tonight. As soon as there's a boy involved, she changes. I always try to be accepting of her when she does this. But tonight—I think I've had enough.

I grab Polly's empty glass and leave them to it. Juliet's in the Bar Room, filling an antique silver champagne bucket with ice. She's singing along to Josephine Baker, but I've got too much on to be annoyed by her. Once I've prepared the drinks, I place them on a wooden tray and carry them to the Red Room.

James has the lights set on Annabelle, and she's posing in front of the red curtains while he snaps away. She looks pretty amazing.

'This is good, Annabelle. You look great,' James tells her. 'I'd really like to do some with all those red vases as the backdrop.'

He looks towards me as I indicate his full glass of beer on the dark oak table. 'Thanks, Joni.'

He said my name! He said my name!

The sound of the front door opening brings with it a gust of icy air. This must be one of the Gatsby twos. I greet them, leave them, check the bookings diary, and then seat them. They look like a husband and wife. Night out while the babysitter minds their two kids at home.

'Just one moment, and I'll bring you some menus,' I tell them, tray under my arm, head turning towards James as I make my way back down the hallway.

When I return with their menus and take their drink orders, I notice James has set up his tripod in the doorway to the Red Room and is shooting towards the vases and urns. Annabelle is staring down the lens, arms above her head, as she works the camera like a born star. I smile at her. How can I be mad at her? She's incredible.

The night rolls on, and I begin to feel as though I'm living in parallel worlds. My Trying-to-Impress-James-in-the-Red-Room world is constantly being disrupted by the world of Serving-the-Ordinary-Customers-in-Gatsby, in whom I have no interest whatsoever. Both Lucy and Dave have given me a 'How's it going?', and I've informed them that there hasn't been any progress with me and James. I updated them with the good news, though: Annabelle has cooled off, and I think she's getting the hint that James is not interested in her.

When the Gatsby customers are onto after-dinner coffees and teas, I hear Polly call out to me. 'Joni, we're sta-arving!' she cries, hanging onto the *ar* sound for an awfully long time. She's a little bit on the tipsy side of town.

I give her a nod, noticing that James is starting to pack up. I panic, because I don't want him to leave.

'James is done, and we're ready to start on the interview,' Polly says excitedly.

'Great,' I tell her. 'Can I help with that?' I ask James, who seems to be about to carry his camera gear out to his car.

'Oh, I'll be right. Thanks though,' he says. 'If it's okay, I might stay for dinner too.'

My heart lights up inside me. 'Of course, of course. That would be . . . lovely. Really . . . wonderful.'

I feel stupid for using the word *wonderful*.

'How are those knees feeling?' he asks.

'Oh!' I look down towards the scrape from earlier on. 'I forgot about that.'

We smile at each other, and then he picks up his heavy

light-stands. I open up the front door for him. He says thanks. It's at this point that I want to touch his shoulder, or his back, or his hair or his face—but I don't.

He walks out into the night-time. I close the door, begin to clear away the dirty glasses in the Red Room, and await his return.

19

'Menus,' I say, placing three on the table in front of Annabelle and Polly.

'Lovely,' Polly chimes. 'Is James joining us?'

James overhears as he wanders back into the Red Room. 'Maybe I'll leave you ladies to it,' he tells them. Then he turns to me, taking me by surprise. 'I might come and sit out the back. Do you think that sounds okay?'

'Oh yeah. Sure, sure. That's a great idea,' I say casually.

'Hey Joni, are there any specials?' Annabelle asks.

By this stage, her drunkenness has worn off a little. She's read the rejection signs from James, eased up on the flirting, and reverted to the kinder Annabelle—the Annabelle I love.

'Ah yes,' I tell her. 'The special tonight is *coq au vin*.' I'm so embarrassed saying *cock* in front of James.

Annabelle laughs. 'What's *coq au vin*?'

I blush. 'Chicken braised in red wine.'

'That sounds great,' James says. 'I'll have that, please.'

'Make that two cocks,' Annabelle says, in her cutesy voice.

'Ah, ha,' Polly ding-dongs on each syllable. 'Three cocks, Joni. Cock times three!'

We all have a giggle.

'And I'll bring some parsley potatoes and a side of peas. How does that sound?'

'Marvellous,' Polly says, shuffling her notepad around, then picking up her mini tape-recorder in preparation for interviewing Annabelle.

I look at James. 'Do you want to . . .'

'Come out the back with you?'

'Um . . . yes. That . . . that's what I was going to suggest.'

I turn and notice the last remaining couple in Gatsby are signalling me for the bill, and I acknowledge their request with a nod. Then James and I head for the Bar Room past the ladies in Lillibon, who are all devouring their desserts.

'Do you want to sit down here?' I ask him. 'Dave!' I call out towards the kitchen, and Dave springs out into the Bar Room. 'Dave, this is James.'

Dave wipes his greasy hand on his pants and gives James a firm, friendly handshake. 'Hey mate, how's it going? Are you the photographer?'

I leave them to chat. On my way to get the bill ready for the Gatsby couple, I find Lucy already preparing it.

'I'll do this,' she tells me. 'And I'll take care of Lillibon. You talk to James. Go, go! Take your apron off. Have a drink. Loosen up.'

'Okay.' Then, shit, I realise I need to give Dave the food order. He beats me to it.

'Joni, have you got their order there in your hot little hand,' he asks, making me feel self-conscious. 'I'm sure James here is pretty hungry.'

'Yep.' I hand him their order.

'Oooh, *coq au vin*,' Dave says playfully, in his most over-the-top French accent.

James laughs. I knew he'd like Dave.

I untie my apron. James watches me, his mouth forming the beginnings of a smile. It feels wonderful, him watching me. But I feel quite shy around him, so I look down at the floorboards, then place my dirty apron in the basket.

'Can I get you another drink?' I ask him.

'You know, I feel like a coffee. Would that be okay?'

'Sure.' I walk over to the coffee machine, worrying that he's a total coffee snob and will hate the burnt-tasting coffee I'll make for him. 'What kind of coffee do you like?'

'Long black, thanks,' he says, looking out the back window. 'That cat is so beautiful. I love the colours in her coat.'

'That's Tiger-Lily, the Harland cat.'

I set his coffee going and turn towards him. I notice his eyes moving from Tiger-Lily to the quaint deer ornaments on the windowsill; across the elaborately framed oil paintings Lucy has picked up at markets here and there; then up to the two brass wall-lamp holders—both of them shaped like naked women, with their arms stretched up high, holding rosy-pink lampshades.

'I love it here,' he tells me.

'Me too.'

'You know how I'd describe this place?'

'How?'

'Lovesome,' James says, looking me right in my eyes.

'What's lovesome?' I ask, hoping I don't sound uneducated.

'Lovely,' he tells me, in his warm-sounding voice.

That's what you are, James. That's what you are. Lovesome.

'How long have you worked here?' he asks me.

'About six months.'

I pull out a saucer, place his full coffee cup on it, and rest it in front of him.

He smells the coffee up close. 'Nothing like a hot cup of Joe,' he says jokingly.

My mind wanders straight into an episode of *Twin Peaks*, with Dale Cooper in the Double R Diner, though I'm not sure if that's what he's referencing. I watch his mouth as he takes a sip.

'That's a damn fine cup of coffee,' he says, definitely impersonating Agent Cooper now.

I give him a smile. 'I love *Twin Peaks*.'

'Me too,' he says, watching me stand and reach for a bottle of red wine on the top shelf. 'You know, I went to the real Double R Diner, where they filmed the show. Well, the exterior shots.' James takes another sip of his coffee. 'Last year. With one of my best mates, Brett.'

'Oh.' I fill my wine glass and return to the staff table, sitting near him at the same corner.

'Brett had this nightmare of a girlfriend. Diane. Can you believe her name was Diane?'

'Diane, like the Diane Agent Cooper spoke to on his dictaphone every night?' Dave asks, exiting the kitchen holding three dinner plates piled with *coq au vin*.

'Yeah,' James tells us.

Dave, who's obviously been listening to our entire conversation, places a plate in front of James and I walk quickly into the hallway to grab him some cutlery from the sideboard.

'Thanks, Dave. This looks amazing!' James exclaims.

Dave disappears, delivering the other two plates to Annabelle and Polly in the Red Room.

'Would you like a wine with your dinner?' I ask James.

'Oh . . . just a small glass, thanks.' He stares down at his full plate, looking immensely happy.

'Red or white?'

'Actually, on second thoughts I'll just have water.'

I immediately feel like an alcoholic. I walk in shame to the bar, fill an amber drinking glass with water and place it beside James's plate. 'Here.'

'Thanks.' His head tilts back as he takes a long sip, and his neck stretches beautifully. 'So, yeah—Diane, this girlfriend of Brett's,' he continues.

'Hang on—where *is* the Double R Diner?' I ask him.

'It's in Washington state.' He eats a button mushroom, and I love the way his face moves. 'The actual diner from the outside looked amazing. And then we wandered inside, with all these other tourists, and then Diane sort of went crazy.'

'What do you mean?'

'Well, we sat at one of the booths. It was actually kind of depressing—none of the small-town charm I was expecting. I wanted there to be smooth, wonky music in the background, for Shelly to walk out from behind the counter, for Coop to be drinking coffee at the bar, the Log Lady sitting in the corner. You know, exactly like the show. For some stupid reason I'd romanticised the whole thing before we got there.'

'Did you have some cherry pie?' I ask him.

'Yeah, well,' he laughs, before taking a mouthful.

'Sorry—you eat,' I say.

He swallows, quickly.

'So. We were inside, we got the booth seat. I said that already, didn't I?' James's face becomes more animated. 'Then an incredibly rude waitress came and served us. Nothing like you, of course. The lighting was terrible. Nothing like the show,' he says. 'I mean, I love colour, and all the warmth of the interiors on the show.'

'Me too.'

'The reds. It's so heavy with red, isn't it? You know, all the flashing signage. I love that about *Twin Peaks*.'

'Me too.'

'So anyway.' He puts more food in his mouth and chews and swallows, and I watch him, as a warm, funny feeling weaves through my tummy. This is so nice. He's paying so much attention to me. And he likes what I like. 'So finally we get into a booth,' he tells me.

He's already said they were in the booth, but I don't say anything, because he's too adorable. The more he talks, the more he awakens amusement and pleasure within me. I'm captivated by his muddled-up delivery. Maybe he's nervous, talking to me. I think that's it! He's stuffing up the story because he's nervous!

'Oh, and the colour scheme was totally washed out. Fluorescent lighting, and sort of dull. A terribly unflattering wash.'

I love that he experiences the world through how the light falls around him. A true photographer.

'And the floor was dirty, but not in a good way—old dirty. Disgusting dirty. Grotty. You know what I mean?'

'Yeah, I know what you mean,' I tell him, not just pretending to agree, but really knowing what he means.

'So anyway, we order cherry pie. I mean, we can't go there without ordering the Twin Peaks classic. So the pie comes to the table, with three damn fine cups of coffee, and then Diane has one mouthful, and . . . I admit the pie was pretty poor, not how you'd imagine it would taste on the show, when you're watching it. So yeah, Brett says some small thing to Diane, something about a lunch they'd had at their place, and Diane goes nuts. She goes in for this long-winded monologue about Brett and how he leaves his dirty underwear on the floor, and how she can't stand him, and how it's all over. And then she storms out, and gets in her car and drives off. You see, she drove—she'd driven us all there. So Brett and I, we're stranded at the Double R Diner. Well it's actually called Twede's Diner in real life. So we're at Twede's. And then . . . Sorry, this story isn't really going anywhere.'

'No, it is. I like where it's going. Keep going,' I tell him, sipping my wine, then excitedly tucking my hands under my legs, and sitting on them. James eats the food off his fork.

'Okay. So Brett has to find someone to give us a lift back to Seattle, and . . . I don't know. That's enough about my Double R Diner story. What about you? Tell me about you. Did you go to Mosman High? You look familiar.'

'No.'

I adore him, and love his story, even if he thinks it fizzled out and didn't really go anywhere. In fact it's the most beautiful story that didn't go anywhere that I've ever heard.

'I grew up around and about,' I say, feeling more and more comfortable in his presence. 'Mainly in Glebe. Where do you live?'

'I'm actually living on a boat at the moment. Bit illegal. Maybe?' He gives me a cheeky grin.

'Wow! In Sydney?'

Please live in Sydney. Please live in Sydney.

'Yeah, it's moored up in Pittwater. It's my parents' boat, and . . . I don't know, I travel quite a bit with work, so it kind of suits me to have a boat as my house. Is that weird?'

'I like weird,' I tell him. 'But that's not weird. I mean, it's the kind of weird I love.'

We sit quietly for a moment while he eats and ingests my love of weirdness. Then my mind conjures up the worst-case scenario—I imagine him on his yacht in his pyjamas with his girlfriend in a bikini diving off the front of the boat, and then James diving in after her and swimming up to her and pashing her like crazy.

'Bit lonely on there sometimes, though,' he says, looking into my eyes as though he's a little boy.

'Oh, you live by yourself?'

'By myself. How 'bout you? Do you—'

'By myself. I don't have a boyfriend.' *Joni, you idiot.*

'I haven't had a girlfriend for a while. This feels like a date. Does this feel like a date to you? In . . . a good way?'

Oh my god, I love that he thinks this feels like a date.

'Um . . . sort of.'

Juliet bursts into the room through the back door.

'Guys! My Pines people are coming through. No smoking, no swearing, no stripping!'

I look at James, feeling responsible for Juliet's outfit, hair-do and humour. Although that was pretty funny. James chuckles, and gives me a *who is this nutcase* look.

I take James's empty plate and coffee cup up to the bench.

'Thank you,' he says, following me up.

I stand beside him, and try to lean into him a little bit.

I wobble over, holding onto one of his shoulders. He puts his arm around my waist, just for the tiniest splice of a moment, and I smell his smell. Not aftershave, but his *smell*.

I inhale him, and I can't get enough. I feel like holding him in my arms for hours. Cocooning myself in his strong body and looking into his funny face, listening to stories about Diane and cherry pie.

The corporate-looking group from the Pines walk into the Bar Room one by one. Gone is the perfect make-up. Gone are the perfect postures. Instead, it's all rosy cheeks and slouchy stumbles, followed by the sound of handbags falling off shoulders. I look at James.

'Do you want to come with me?' he asks quietly.

'Where?'

We're whispering like kids in a dark cupboard playing hide-and-seek.

'I want to take some long-exposure photos tonight. Maybe down at the wharf. End of Darling Street. Is that weird? Me asking you to come along?'

'No. That's not weird, even though . . .'

'. . . you like weird.' He finishes my sentence and we look into each other's eyes and I feel like I've found him. I've found my guy.

'Yes. I'd love to come with you,' I tell him, the rumble and chatter of the Pines crowd passing through the room bubbling away in the background.

'Let's go now. Shall we? Or do you have to stay and clean up?'

'Let me check with Lucy.'

20

Walking through Harland in search of Lucy, I smile at everything I see. The cuckoo clock in Lillibon, the old gold cash
register on the hallway sideboard, the fireplace in Gatsby. When
I enter the Red Room, there's no Lucy, just Polly and Annabelle,
deep in conversation. I study Annabelle closely. Her puffed-up
bleached blonde hair. Her pale skin, blue eyes—like sapphires.
She's leaning one elbow on the table, and her brow is furrowed
as she quietly confesses something or other to Polly. The longer I
look at her, the louder becomes the voice inside my head, telling
me that, *finally*, someone has picked me.

*James just asked me to go somewhere with him, and he didn't
ask you to go anywhere with him, and he didn't tell you anything
about the Double R Diner, and he didn't put his arm around your
waist, but he kind of put his arm around mine, and . . .*

'Joni!' Annabelle calls to me warmly, reaching her arm out,
inviting me to hold her hand. 'I just told Polly everything about
me and Johnny, and how he broke up with me over the phone
today.'

'I'm not going to print it, of course,' Polly tells me, although I bet she will.

'I told Polly how you and I met at my second live show ever.'

'That's so cool,' Polly says, placing her fork in line with the knife on her empty plate.

'Yeah, we're such good friends,' I tell Polly.

'The best,' gushes Annabelle.

Stretching my arm out, I take Annabelle's hand. We hold tight. I know this grip so well. But I'm only vaguely absorbing what they're saying, 'cause I'm overwhelmed by the mysterious chemistry that's developing between me and James.

'Can I get you guys some dessert?' I ask them.

'I'm right, thanks,' Annabelle says.

'I'm full to the brim. Right up to here.' Polly puts on a silly face and points to the top of her forehead.

And then the dingle of the bells on the front door brings with it the smell of Lucy's perfume, and I let go of Annabelle's hand. 'I just need to ask Lucy something. You two carry on.'

Polly looks at Annabelle. 'Okay. So, your next record. Have you started writing for that yet? Or are you still in touring mode?'

I leave them be.

'Lucy,' I say quietly, putting my hand on her shoulder.

Together we walk into Gatsby. The room is people-free. Only chairs, and tables with empty, stained coffee cups on them. Lucy busies herself with tidying up.

'How is everything going out there?' she asks.

'Really good,' I tell her excitedly. 'James just asked me to hang out with him. Tonight! He's wondering if I can knock off now.'

'What!' Lucy's face lights up.

'I know! Can you believe it?'

'Oh my god. Yes. Finish up now. I'll clean up.'

'Really?'

'*Oui.*'

She reaches out to me and hugs me tight. Then she holds my shoulders firmly, and stares intensely into my eyes. 'The only way to love is deeply and completely. So much so that one begins to experience a sense of madness. For all true lovers know that there is no love without madness.'

I'm mesmerised by her passionate words. Her French accent. Her emphasis on the word *madness*.

'That's beautiful. Did you make that up?'

'No. Maman used to say it to me whenever I met a new boy I liked. She was extremely dramatic. We clashed. Too similar.'

James wanders into Gatsby, hands in his pockets. I smile at him.

'You two heading off now?' Lucy says, as though she's my mum.

'Ah, yeah,' James tells her casually. 'I might just say goodbye to Polly and Annabelle before we go.'

'Me too.'

'I'm just wondering . . .' Lucy says, leading us into the Red Room. Polly and Annabelle look up towards her.

'I'm just wondering,' Lucy repeats, 'if Polly and James might like to join us at the staff dinner this Wednesday night. We have caterers coming. There'll be plenty of food. And, you know, you've come all the way from London, Polly. And James, it would be lovely to have you here. Could be nice to get a few photos during the night. I can pay you, of course.'

I can't believe she's helping me out like this.

Lucy continues, 'We have a sit-down dinner, and a little dancing, and cocktails—lots of wine. I usually invite a few extras. Spice things up a bit.'

Polly looks excited. 'That sounds like so much fun, and I don't fly back to London until Friday, so I'm in!'

'I'd love to come too,' James says, looking right at me.

'Annabelle's coming, aren't you?' Lucy checks.

'Yeah, yeah.' Annabelle's tone of voice suggests that she's not that interested in joining us. I imagine it's because it's becoming obvious that something is brewing between me and James. But if Polly's coming, she'll definitely want to be here. She won't want to appear like a party pooper in the UK press.

'Great. That's sorted,' Lucy says, in punchy staccato.

'Shall we go, then?' James asks me.

'Yeah.'

Annabelle gives me an envious, extra-long stare. 'Where are you two off to?'

'Down to the wharf. Taking some photos. We'll see you all Wednesday?' James keeps it short and sweet.

'Yes, darling,' Polly says, rising from her chair and walking towards James. She gives him an air-kiss on each cheek.

Annabelle breaks her competitive stare. 'We're heading up to the Emerald after this, if you two want to join us?'

'Um, maybe,' I tell her.

Lucy starts to clear the table and the interview resumes as James and I walk back into the Bar Room. I grab my things, put my jumper on, and poke my head into the kitchen to say goodbye to Michael and Dave.

'See ya, Joni!' Dave calls, then walks out from the kitchen. 'Great to meet you, James,' he says with pep.

'Likewise,' James says, as they shake hands.

'Let's go,' I tell James. 'This way.' I hoist the straps of my backpack over each shoulder and lead him out through the back door. It's dark and cold as we walk down the side path. As per usual, the golden glow from the window next door lights up Harland's white weatherboards. I bet James is thinking about how beautiful the lighting is.

'I just want to get my camera out of my car,' he tells me.

We walk towards an old station wagon parked under the streetlight out the front of Harland. James unlocks the door on the passenger side, and pulls out his camera and a tripod.

'Do you live near here?' he asks me, putting his camera strap over his shoulder.

'Yeah, just down Darling Street, and then you take a right turn and . . . it's up in that area.' I point towards where I think my place is. 'I ride my bike in,' I tell him as we start to walk down the middle of Darling Street towards the wharf. There aren't any cars at this time of night. It's quiet, and still.

'Was that your cute little bike leaning against the shed?'

'Yeah.'

I begin to give him more information about myself, even though he's not asking for it. 'I usually head into work at about five. But I paint during the day. I'm . . . I'm an artist.'

'I thought you might be,' he says, with a smile.

'What made you think that?'

'I don't know. I just . . . thought you might be. I feel as if I know you. Like we went to primary school together, or something.'

'I sort of have that feeling too,' I tell him.

We walk downhill together, getting closer to the wharf. We pass parked cars, the sandstone cottages and terrace houses, and a bus parked at the stop. It won't start moving until the next ferry comes in, and then it will drive all the passengers home.

'Do you study art?' James asks me.

'Yeah, I studied at Sydney College of the Arts. I graduated last year, a few weeks before my twenty-first birthday.'

'Joni, you're a baby,' he says, poking fun at me.

'What? I'm not a baby. How old are you?'

'Twenty-seven.'

'And did you study?'

'Nope. Self-taught. I travelled a lot after I left school. Got any more questions?' he says playfully. 'Ask me one, and then I'll ask you one, until we get up to ten.'

'Okay.' I gladly play along. 'So you live on your parents' boat—do they live in Sydney?'

'Yep. My go. Favourite food?' He turns to look at me with soft eyes as we start to walk over to the left-hand side of the road.

'Favourite food? Um . . . chocolate. Actually, no. I'm gonna say almond croissants. What about you? What's your favourite food?'

'Um . . . spanakopita.'

'Spana what?'

'Spanakopita. It's Greek. Come on!' He snaps his fingers repeatedly. 'Fast game's a good game.'

He jumps up on the knee-high sandstone wall that surrounds the garden bed at the side of the footpath.

'Okay, okay,' I tell him, following him up onto the wall. He walks quickly along the top, almost running, as though he's begging me to chase him.

'First job!' I call out to him, almost losing my balance trying to keep up.

'Delivering newspapers on my BMX!'

We both laugh. James jumps down when he gets to the end of the wall, and runs towards the large grassy park that sits hard up against the water's edge. He has the spirit of a child in the body of a man. And his mind—I still can't place it in any category. Who is this guy? A dreamer *and* a doer? I just want to get inside his head. I want to know everything he thinks, everything he feels.

I catch up to him, and we stand together, staring out at the Harbour Bridge. It's lit up, in full view, and it looks grand and glorious, rising tall above the dark water that flips and flops and bobs and bangs into the boats and sandstone bricks surrounding the harbour. That large body of water. The constant movement. The flickering, reflected lights. It's a part of who I am. What I'm made of. Where I come from. James looks at me, and I wonder whether he might try to kiss me.

'Do you have any brothers or sisters?' he asks.

'No. I'm an only child. You?'

'Two sisters,' he says. 'Favourite artist?'

'Mmm.' I think carefully. 'I can't name just one, so I'm going to throw a few at you. Klee, Egon Schiele . . . um . . . it's a bit of a man's world, isn't it, when it comes to art. I can't think of any women. I mean, there's Cindy Sherman. She's great. Judy Chicago . . .'

'Okay, I'll give you a woman. She's my favourite photographer. Julia Margaret Cameron. Her portraits are beautiful. Have you heard of her?'

'No, never.'

'She was around in the mid-to-late eighteen hundreds. She took a lot of close, cropped portraits of Victorian celebrities. I went and visited her house on the Isle of Wight. She used the wet collodion process and . . .'

'Is that like an old photographic technique?'

'Yeah. But her portraits are in soft focus, and at the time people thought they looked like mistakes. But really she was intentionally creating these beautiful, blurry artworks. They were more like black-and-white or sepia-toned paintings.'

'Wow, I'd love to see some of her work.'

James quickly puts his tripod down and holds onto both of my shoulders. He twists my body gently, so my back is facing the water.

'Stand here,' he orders, setting up his tripod. 'Don't move.'

'What? I . . .'

'There's a ferry coming. I'm going to take a long-exposure photo of you,' he tells me, attaching his camera to the tripod and bending to look through the viewfinder. 'You need to stay really still. I'm going to have the shutter open for about thirty seconds. The ferry's coming in towards the wharf, and it's going to make a pretty line behind you.'

'Okay,' I tell him, keeping as still as I can.

He presses the button on the camera gently, then looks at me. We stand silently for ten seconds or so.

'Don't laugh, don't laugh,' he says, on the edge of laughter himself.

I can't hold it in anymore. I start to giggle. 'Stop it. You're making me laugh,' I tell him. 'Look. I'm moving, I'm moving. And now I'm talking. My mouth's going to be blurry, isn't it? Are we making art? Is this going to be one giant mistake?'

'One giant mistake of a photo,' James says, sarcastically. 'Pure art.'

I try to settle my giggles, and then James announces: 'Okay, done. Can I—'

'Race you to the swings!' I bolt as fast as I can, over to the two swings in the grassy playground, and James follows, leaving his camera behind. I jump on a swing and begin to push myself up, back and forth, as high as I can. He watches me, then jumps on the other swing and tries to propel himself higher than me.

'Favourite poet?' he calls out.

'What?' I yell back.

'Who's your favourite poet?'

I let my swing slow down, gradually, gradually, and James does the same. We swing low, and I tell him: 'Keats.'

James recites with veritable passion: '*My heart aches . . .*'

Together in unison we declare, '*and a drowsy numbness pains my sense . . .*'

'*As though of hemlock I had drunk,*' I finish.

'Oh,' James says. 'I couldn't remember that bit.'

We both hang from the cold chains of the swings, twisting, spinning side to side.

'What about Allen Ginsberg?' James leans over closer, and touches my boots with the tips of his.

Our knees bump into each other. I don't pull back; instead, I move forward, and our knees bump together again. I look into his dark-brown eyes.

'I haven't read much Allen Ginsberg.'

'I have one of his books in my car. I'll lend it to you.'

*

After he packs up his camera, we wander back up to Harland. James asks me all about my work and my influences. He tells me my paintings sound incredible, and that he'd love to come and see them. When we reach his car, he unlocks the passenger-side door and puts his camera gear on the front seat. Then he opens up the glove box and pulls out a little book with a black and white cover: 'Howl' by Allen Ginsberg.

'I love how you keep it in your glove box,' I tell him.

'Well, you never know when you might need a bit of poetry,' he jokes. 'At home . . . out on the road . . .'

I can't help but laugh.

He tenderly places the book in my hand. 'For you.'

'Thank you.' I pause. 'Well, I guess I should get going. I've gotta ride home. So you'll be at the—'

'Can I get your phone number?'

'Oh. Of course you can. But you'll be at the dinner on Wednesday night, won't you?'

'Yeah. But can I get your phone number now?' He smiles at me, then reaches into his car and pulls out a pen. 'You should come and have lunch with me on my boat one day.'

'I'd like that,' I say.

We exchange numbers, we say goodbye, and I walk down the side path to get my bike while James climbs into his car and drives off. No kiss, no hug, just an overwhelming feeling of anticipation.

21

Taking the downhill run on Darling Street at a dangerous speed, I call out into the night: 'Aaaaaaaah!' And then the silence that follows, in stark contrast with my uncontrollable outburst, brings with it a clean freshness. That winter chill, hanging over the rooftops and winding narrow streets.

My cheeks begin to hurt, because I'm smiling so hugely. I stretch my neck up, and show my smile to the stars that glitter in the pitch-black sky. But then my front tyre gets the wobbles, so I grab the handlebars tighter and, thank God, save myself from a potentially disastrous stack.

I pull into my street and jump off my bike, still smiling, big and radiant. Up on the footpath, wheeling my bike along, I notice that the side gate is slightly ajar. Annabelle mustn't have closed it properly, but who cares—I'm so glad she's home. I can't wait to tell her everything. Rushing in, I lean my bike against the side of my bungalow, and skip up the stairs. I knock quietly, knowing she'll answer, and I'll be inside faster than if I fish around for my keys in my backpack.

The door opens. 'Hi Joni.'

Oh, weird—it's Michael, of all people.

'Hey Joni!' Annabelle calls from the kitchenette. 'We were just up at the Emerald, and it was last drinks, so we're back here. You want a drink?'

'Nah, I'm gonna have a cup of tea.'

I wander in, feeling a little strange that Michael is at my place. He sits down at the table—*my* table—opposite Annabelle, who picks up from where she must have left off, partway through a story about a concert she played on her recent UK tour. They've helped themselves to the red wine I bought yesterday, and the chocolates I planned to give Lucy at the staff dinner.

I take my backpack off and drop it near the door. Annabelle's suitcase is wide open on the floor near the couch, her clothes (and those of mine that she's borrowed) almost covering the entire floor of my bungalow. It's been like this for weeks, but it hasn't irritated me until now.

Annabelle's concert story comes to an end, and as I'm filling the kettle with water, I ask them, 'How was the Emerald?'

'Yeah, fine,' Annabelle says, holding her wine glass with both hands. 'How 'bout you? Where did you guys go? Come on, spill the beans.'

Her voice contains a mix of excitement at my good fortune with a suggestion of envy. I'm confused by her intentions, and can't quite read how to move forward with the conversation. Her body language suggests she wants to include me in her drinking and late-night storytelling with Michael, so I sit down next to her and proceed with caution, deciding I'll keep the more intimate details to myself.

'We went down to the wharf and hung out for a bit.'

I downplay the whole thing—the obvious shared attraction and chemistry between me and James—but I question myself as I'm doing it. I'm usually so open with Annabelle. I usually tell her everything. *Everything*. But I'm still hurt by the fact that she flirted with James and tried to win him over, even though she already knew I had the hots for him. Although . . . did meeting him first give me the right to pursue him, and Annabelle no right to make a move?

It's a blurred line within any friendship. And now Michael— what's he doing here?

'Is James coming to the staff dinner?' Annabelle asks me.

'Yeah. He asked for my phone number too.'

'What! Joni! That's huge! Oh my god, he likes you!' She sounds happy for me. Free of nastiness.

Now I can't hold back my excitement. I pretend that Michael's not here, and talk only to Annabelle. 'We have so much in common. He lives on a boat, and he invited me to come for lunch on it! He lent me a book. He feels like he knows me from his childhood. He wants to come and see my paintings. He took a photo of me—'

'He took lots of photos of me tonight,' Annabelle blurts out.

I sink into my seat. Her jealous side has reared its ugly head again, and I regret having told her anything.

'Sounds like you two might get it on,' she says, looking at Michael and raising her eyebrows.

Get it on? I find that offensive. I'm at the beginning of falling for someone, the beginning of finding out what's inside a beautiful man's mind. Where's the Annabelle who wants the best for me, and understands me completely?

'Maybe. Maybe we'll get it on,' I tell her, nonchalantly,

shrugging my shoulders and trying to act cool. I get up to make myself a chamomile tea, thinking how disappointed I am with her.

'So anyway . . .' Annabelle continues talking to Michael only, excluding me from the conversation. I can't handle her when she's like this. She's bouncing back and forth from understanding friend to jealous competitor.

The smell of the chamomile flowers soaking in my teapot fills the kitchen. It overpowers the stink of alcohol, and Annabelle's mix of smoke and perfume, and Michael's greasy T-shirt. The same stained T-shirt he cooked in all night. I don't wanna get ready for bed while Michael's still here, but then again it might give him the message that I want him to leave my house, now. I hide in the bathroom with my cup of tea, and take a shower.

When I get out and walk through the living area, wrapped in my towel, Michael glances at me. I climb the ladder stairs up to my bed and slip into an oversized T-shirt and undies, making sure they can't see me. I leave the wet towel at the end of my mattress.

'Night!' I call out.

They don't reply.

'Goodnight, you two!' I say a little louder.

'Oh, night Joni,' Annabelle says. 'Are we too loud?'

'Um, sort of. I'm really tired. I wanna get some sleep.' I don't care if I sound rude.

'Let's go out on the front verandah, Michael. Here, take this.'

I look down, and see Annabelle pulling up the crocheted rug from the couch and grabbing her faux fur black coat. She puts a ciggie between her lips, and somehow manages to talk at the same time.

'Want one?' she asks Michael.

'I don't smoke, but thanks,' he says quietly.

I peer down as they walk out the front door, leaving it slightly ajar. On their way out, Annabelle puts her arm around Michael's waist. Great. I can see where this is going. She better go back to his house, or I'm seriously gonna lose it. Their outdoor chitter-chatter still makes its way up to my mezzanine-level bed, but my thoughts of James soon block out their annoying small talk. I blissfully relive all the main moments of our time together. James and I on the swings. James running along the stone wall. James taking my photo. James touching my boots with his. And then I drift off to sleep.

It feels like only seconds later that I'm awakened by a strange noise. I wonder if there's a possum outside, up in the gum tree, letting out a disturbing mating call. Then I realise it's worse than that. Much worse.

The animal-like moan is overtaken by a groan. Bare skin slapping against bare skin makes a repetitive clapping sound. It's disgusting and, now that I'm fully awake, it's perfectly clear to me that Annabelle and Michael are in the middle of having sex on my couch. I roll over and let out an exaggerated sigh, hoping they'll remember that I'm up here, only a few metres away from them.

But they continue as if they're in a soundproof recording studio, which I can guarantee has already been a love-making location Annabelle has ticked off her list. This is so gross. I haven't heard her have sex before, and now I know she is extremely loud while in the act.

I roll over and block my ears. This is never happening again. I want her out of here. Tomorrow. I lie awake until Annabelle very obviously climaxes and Michael, in true Michael style, reaches his peak quietly.

Sunshine is filtering through the curtains when I wake. I sit up and check out the scene below. Annabelle is curled up on the floor, and Michael is lying long on the couch. At least she's been a lady and given him the bed. Aside from that, pretty much everything she's done in the last twelve hours has been atrocious. I bet she's hungover like crazy.

I shuffle down to the end of my bed and descend the ladder stairs, unsure if it's better for me to intentionally wake them, or aim to keep them sleeping. As soon as I land on the floor Annabelle wakes.

'Joni,' she says in a croaky voice, followed by a yawn. 'Did we keep you awake?'

I go in hard. 'I'm gonna make a coffee. And then can I talk to you outside?'

'Sure. What is it?'

'Just let me grab a coffee first. You want one?'

'Yes please,' she says, midway through an even bigger yawn than the first.

She stumbles over to the bathroom, and I hear her wee trickle into the toilet as I screw the coffee pot together. She could have had the decency to close the door. I place the pot on a hot plate and walk past her as she leaves the bathroom, and I enter.

Once I'm done, I pour out two coffees, adding milk to both. I take my dressing gown off the hook, and meet Annabelle out on the front verandah. She's rugged up in her black faux fur coat. Her hair is in one giant fluff knot, and her mascara has run down her cheeks. She smells like sex, vanilla, body odour and liquor. She lights up a ciggie, adding a smoky stench to the mix.

'So,' I begin, 'it's not cool that you brought Michael home last night.'

'What? I thought you'd be totally fine with that.' She is straight-out offended and defensive. 'Especially after what happened to me yesterday. I mean, fuck, Joni. I got dumped over the phone, I had to put on a show for Polly, and be interviewed and charming, *and* have my photo taken for a massive magazine.' She sips her coffee and then rudely adds, 'While *you* ran off with the goddamned photographer.' She puffs, and blows out smoke. 'Who was, by the way, trying to make a move on me, until you stepped in and stole him from me.'

'What!' I am utterly shocked.

'He was into me, I know it.'

'No he's not, and no he wasn't. You just can't take it that he chose me, can you? And besides, you were the one who was going to try to set me up with the photographer.'

'That was the photographer from London, and before Johnny dumped me.'

Her reasoning is ridiculous.

I hold onto my hot cup of coffee and take a long sip, then stare into the milky surface. Annabelle gazes out into the backyard and does a *tap-tap* with her finger, encouraging the ash from her cigarette to fall onto the verandah floor.

'Well . . .' she offers, sounding unsure of what she'll say next. 'I had a great night with Michael last night, so I have nothing to complain about.'

'I heard you,' I tell her gruffly.

'We moved out onto the verandah. Surely we weren't that loud.'

'I heard you having sex, you idiot.'

'Sorry,' she says. And she looks like she means it.

I decide to ask the question. The one I've wanted to ask her for a long time. 'Why do you just go from boy to boy? You fall in love with one, break up, jump on to someone else. It's not good for you to never be alone. It's like you use every guy to help you get over the one before.'

She stares long and hard at the ground. I sip my coffee, and begin to feel uncomfortable with the long silence.

Finally Annabelle says, 'I need to head out and meet Polly for the second part of the interview. Up at Café Blue. She's still got questions for me.' She pulls her hungover body up off the chair and stumbles towards the door. She turns her head before she's made it inside and says, in a cold, insensitive tone, 'You don't understand me, Joni, and you never have. It's a major flaw in our friendship. I'm gonna take my stuff, and I'll be moving in with Michael, because how I conduct my love life is completely normal, and men love me, and I don't need people like you telling me how I should live. You've never had a proper boyfriend, and you only just lost your virginity. You're the one who needs to ask yourself what's wrong—with yourself.'

She can't quite put the last insult together properly. But still, I'm so hurt.

'Annabelle,' I say, with the hope she'll take back her harsh words.

'You judge me, Joni, and you make me feel like shit. I need you to know that.'

She turns her back on me as I hold in my tears.

After a moment I follow her back inside, where she and Michael are standing, embracing each other and engaging in a long kiss. I clear my throat. Feeling as if I have nowhere to go to get away, I climb up onto my mezzanine bed, open the little window, look out onto the branches of the gum tree, and have a quiet cry. What a bitch.

22

When Annabelle is showered, dressed and on her way up to meet Polly, I pull myself together and head downstairs to get myself some breakfast. The front door is open, and the mid-morning sun brightens the floorboards. Through the open doorway I see Michael, sitting out on the verandah.

He hears me moving about in the kitchen and wanders inside. 'I hope you don't mind,' he says, chewing. 'I helped myself to a piece of toast.'

'Oh no, that's totally fine. Would you like some coffee? Or fruit?'

'Oh, only if it's no trouble. I'm sorry I stayed over last night,' he says, as I hand him a shiny red apple. 'I offered for Annabelle to come back to my place, but she seemed to think it was fine for us to come here. So yeah, sorry.'

I wish he'd stop apologising. 'So Annabelle's moving into your place, I hear?'

'Well, yeah. For the time being. I'm guessing that's good for you. You'll be able to have your place back to yourself. I love it here, by the way. You've made it look so homely. And Annabelle showed me some of your paintings last night.'

'She did, did she?'

'They're really great, Joni.' He sounds like he means it.

'Thanks, Michael. I've . . .' I'm not sure what to say next. 'We haven't really talked that much, have we? I mean, I don't even know how long you've been working at Harland.'

'A few years now,' Michael says. 'I used to work at a restaurant in Glebe.'

'I used to live in Glebe,' I tell him.

We've found common ground, and it's helping me warm to him, slowly. I place the refilled coffee pot on the stove and turn on the electric hot plate.

'Well, yeah, it was nothing like Harland. Pretty bad, actually.'

'How did you meet Dave?'

'My sister and Dave went out, when she was in high school.'

'What!' I realise I'm starting to enjoy my conversation with Michael. 'Dave's never told me that.'

'Yeah, Dave used to come to all our family Christmas dinners. 'Bout three years in a row.'

'That's hilarious.'

'And then she broke up with Dave and started going out with this awful lawyer.'

I begin to realise that Michael is more than a quiet, over-apologising assistant chef who never says anything. We both pull out a chair and sit down at the table, opposite each other, face to face.

'Did you always know you wanted to be a chef?' I ask him.

'Sort of. I grew up in the country, so I thought I'd just take over Dad's farm. He's a sheep farmer.'

'Wow. I don't think I know anyone who farms sheep. No one who runs a farm, actually. Oh, a couple of girls at uni, but I wasn't really friends with them. I don't know if I'd cope living in the country. I'm a city girl.'

The crackling of the coffee brewing rises over the sound of the birds in the yard. I pull out two yellow mugs, the ones Annabelle gave me for my birthday, and steam rises and swirls up under my chin as I fill them.

'Milk?'

'Yes, thanks.'

We continue our chat.

'I went to boarding school in the city,' Michael tells me.

'Oh. Well, that's kind of like growing up in the city. I guess it's half-and-half, would you say?'

'Well, sort of. It's how I started getting into chefing. I never would have known I could be a chef if I'd spent all my time in the country. A decent chef, anyway. More than a bloody cook in a pub.' He lets out a mini-chuckle, then blows gently over the top of his mug to cool his coffee. 'There were heaps of restaurants around my boarding school,' he tells me. 'I got a lot of takeaway on weekends. I started to become passionate about food.'

I can tell that this is hard for him to say, because he's a bit of a blokey bloke and *passionate* is such a feminine word. Feminine in my eyes, anyhow, or is that sexist?

'Then I moved into the city and studied at hospitality school. I'm really happy doing what I'm doing.'

'Well, that's a good thing, isn't it,' I say. 'It's good to live your life doing what you really love, yeah?'

He nods, then takes a noisy bite from his apple. He's a simple guy. Intelligent, but with a simple outlook and simple needs. I think he'd actually be quite good for Annabelle. He's very level. He might balance out her busy mind and complex nature. Although I can't imagine them staying together as a couple for long.

When we finish our coffee, I pick my clothes up off the floor, and move Annabelle's into a messy pile around her suitcase. Without a word, Michael neatly folds Annabelle's skirts and dresses, gently placing them one by one in her case. What a gentleman, tidying up my bungalow, taking care of Annabelle's things.

'I'm gonna head back to my place and get changed,' he tells me. 'What's the time now?' He glances up at the clock. 'Annabelle should be back soon from that interview. Can you tell her I'll meet her here at about one?'

'Yeah, sure,' I tell him, looking at how neatly he's left the rug and cushions on the couch. I say goodbye and, as he walks out the door, I feel better for knowing a bit more about who he is. I like him. He's not my kind of guy, but he's a decent, kind man. My eyes fall on Annabelle's neatly packed suitcase, and I start to feel bad about making her feel bad about bringing Michael back here.

I run my fingers down the strings of her guitar, which leans against the armrest of the couch. Was I too cruel to her this morning? It's hardly being cruel, pointing out that she jumps too quickly from one relationship to the next. And besides, it's the truth.

I pick up her guitar and notice a small notebook halfway under the couch. It must be her songwriting book. I know it's probably filled with private lyrics, verses and chorus ideas. Bending to retrieve it, I feel the thrill of being caught by her.

Me, looking through her songwriting book. She won't be home in ages. I can't not take a look. I'm so curious. I put the guitar down and sit on the lounge.

First page—incredibly messy handwriting: *In nights and on days*. Mmm. Bit abstract. I flick through a few more pages. Ah yeah, here are the lyrics to her last single: 'I Hear You Calling'. All the words are written out like a poem, in pen. Scribbles here and there, big bold handwriting for the chorus. A few more pages in, I come to a page with a heading at the top: *Poems*. She hasn't told me she writes poetry. Although I guess song lyrics are pretty much poetry. I flick two more pages in. *For Joni*.

Wow. A poem called 'For Joni'. She hasn't told me about this. I read it through.

And where sea meets land
I hold the hand
of another
She's like me
Just like me
she sees
constant shades and colours
rising above, slipping through shutters
Quiet now, quiet
through streets with no beginnings, no endings
corners turned, roads crossed
together.

I love you like a child, my love
like a child in a coat
on a school day

with sounds of birds
and gentle breezes
blowing through thoughts and words
entwined like cross-stitch or
hundred-year-old tapestries
Found.
On walls in homes
Side by side
You and I.

How beautiful. *Entwined like cross-stitch. I love you like a child.* I can't believe she wrote this for me. I look closely at her handwriting. The curve of her *u's,* the dots on her *i's*—always slightly to the right of the line.

I feel a tear run down my right cheek. Why did I make her feel bad about her boy-to-boy lifestyle? Almost everyone does it, don't they? Maybe she's right—am I the one who has problems?

I have a quick shower, and get changed into my cream button-up cardigan and blue jeans. Then I cosy up on the couch and read Jung for a while, folding down the corners of a couple of pages I really love and thinking further about the artist statement I'll need to provide for the works in my group show.

My train of thought is broken by the sound of somebody walking across the lawn. I quickly check to see that I've put Annabelle's songwriting book back where I found it. Yes! Thank god.

I look towards my front door as it slowly swings open, and there she is. Annabelle Reed. She looks windswept, and her red lip-stick has worn off a little. She's holding a bunch of multicoloured roses in one hand, the book that she's reading in the other.

'Joni, I'm so sorry,' she says, handing me the roses.

'I know,' I tell her, feeling so relieved. 'I'm sorry too. I said everything all wrong. I know you're not like me, you're different. In a good way, I mean . . . it's good that you fall into relationships really easily and—'

'Yeah, but I envy you, because you're so independent, and it's like you don't need a guy around. I'm hopeless on my own, Joni. You're so right. I do go from guy to guy. It's bad. But Michael's such a sweet guy. Don't you think?'

I nod. 'You're right, he is. I had a nice chat with him this morning. He's gone back to his place. He said he'll be back around one.'

She pulls out a bulky brown paper bag from her backpack. 'I bought us these.'

She opens up the bag to reveal two almond croissants.

'Awww, that's so nice of you. My favourite.'

I'm not going to tell her I found the 'For Joni' poem in her songwriting book. I don't want her to think that I was snooping around, and going through all her stuff. And she'll probably read it to me one day anyway.

'Second part of the interview went well,' Annabelle tells me, reaching for a couple of plates.

I curl into the corner of the couch. 'I really like Polly.'

'Yeah, me too,' Annabelle says, licking her fingers between each word. She brings my plated-up croissant over to me. 'You know she used to work with James a bit in London?'

'Yeah, James told me. You know, I'm sorry if it seemed like I tried to make a move on—'

'Joni, he's yours. I'm sorry I made such a big deal out of that. I was so drunk, and I've got major jealousy issues. I'm trying to work through that with my therapist. She tells me it's good that I have a competitive nature, because that's what's driving me to succeed with my career. But then it fucks all my friendships.'

'Well,' I say, 'not ours. It almost has, but it never does.'

We both sort of laugh, both offer up another round of apologies, both get up and walk towards each other, both hug, and both almost cry.

Then we sit together eating our croissants, enjoying each other's company.

When Michael appears in the doorway, Annabelle walks over to him straight away and kisses him as though they've been going out for months.

Michael, looking terribly self-conscious, turns towards me. 'Hi Joni.'

'Hi Michael. Come in, come in.'

He walks in slowly, with his hands in his pockets. His black boots are super scuffed up, and his slightly falling-apart brown jumper hangs long over his dark blue jeans. Before I can offer him a drink or a cup of tea, Annabelle says, 'Let me just chuck this stuff in my bag.'

She leans over and grabs her fluffy cardigan. I feel my tummy drop as though I'm about to be caught out for telling a lie to my mum, as Annabelle reaches over the arm of the lounge in search of her songwriting book. My eyes awkwardly dart this way and that, until they rest on Michael, who's checking out Annabelle's legs and lower back as her tight-cropped jumper rises, revealing her perfect porcelain skin.

After sliding her songwriting book into her bag, she reaches for her black faux fur coat. Then she runs into the bathroom. I head towards the kitchen, tidying up a little, while Michael stands patiently waiting for Annabelle.

His tolerant stance reminds me of when I was shopping in the bra and underwear section of a department store once, noting the dominant girls who'd dragged their boyfriends along with them. They left their boys standing awkwardly, surrounded by strapless bras, skin-coloured undies, and high-cut lace teddies, while they spent long stretches of time in the fitting rooms, trying on lingerie. I can see this happening in the Annabelle and Michael partnership.

Suddenly the sound of perfume bottles and cream pots and lipsticks, all falling onto the tiled floor, rattles the submissive energy that Michael has brought into the bungalow.

'Shit!' Annabelle cries out. 'Sorry, guys! Bloody hell.'

Michael and I can't help but have a little laugh. I look into the bathroom, where Annabelle's on all fours, collecting her toiletries.

'Okay, Michael. I'm ready. We can head off!' she calls.

'I'll see you guys to the gate,' I tell them.

Michael, with Annabelle's big suitcase in his hand, leads the way down the stairs. Annabelle, close behind, carries her coat and make-up bag.

When we reach the gate, Annabelle drops her things and gives me a huge, warm embrace. 'Thanks, Joni,' she says softly, her lips right up close to my ear.

'I'm going to miss having you here,' I tell her, thinking, *Well . . . sort of. I love you, but I'm excited about having my place to myself again.*

Michael opens the latch to the gate, and offers a polite goodbye.

'See ya Michael, bye Annabelle. Oh yeah, guys, Wednesday night, I'll see you both at the staff dinner.'

'Ha ha, forgot about that,' Annabelle tells me. 'See ya there, Joni,' she adds excitedly.

I'm happy to hear that's she's psyched about coming to the Harland staff dinner.

I wander back inside and the stillness of my bungalow hangs over my couch, my easel, my painting . . . oh, and Annabelle's guitar. She's left it here!

I clutch it by the neck, and half run down the steps and across the leafy lawn and out the gate. No sign of Annabelle and Michael. They must have driven off in Michael's car.

I walk slowly back towards my bungalow, imagining Annabelle and Michael sitting in the front seats of his car. I wonder if James will pick me up in his car one day.

I hear my phone ringing.

I race in through the front door, place Annabelle's guitar on my couch, and grab the receiver.

'Hello?'

'Is that Joni?'

Oh my god is this James?

'Yes?'

'It's James.'

A bolt of nervous energy rocks my body.

'Oh hi. What are you up to?' I ask him, trying to hide the surprise in my voice. I can't believe he's called me!

'I'm just at the lab dropping off the film from last night. I've been thinking about you, and . . . I'd—I wanted to see if you'd like to have lunch with me.'

'Um, now?'

'Well, I'm not able to now,' he tells me, 'as much as I'd really like to come and have lunch with you now.'

I sort of giggle.

'Tomorrow?' he asks me.

'I'd really like that,' I say, thinking *I cannot believe that you've called me, and I cannot believe that you just asked me out on a lunch date!* The lunch date is (so Annabelle tells me) more romantic than a dinner date.

'How about we have lunch at a café?' James suggests. 'In Balmain?'

'Um, yeah. How about Café Blue? It's close to my place, and . . .'

'I know the one. Shall we say midday? Is that an okay—'

'Midday is great!'

'Well . . .' he says.

I hear the guys at the photo lab talking in the background, and what I think is the Breeders on the radio.

'What are you up to today?' he asks eventually.

I draw a blank. *What am I up to? What am I up to?*

'I'm just going to paint today,' I finally say.

'Aww, that sounds great,' he tells me, making me feel as though he understands me completely.

We both go quiet for a while, and then he says: 'So I'll see you tomorrow?'

'Yes,' I tell him eagerly. 'I'm . . . really looking forward to seeing you again.'

'Me too,' he says.

After I ever so gently put the phone back on the hook, I gaze over towards my couch and books and studio corner, looking at nothing in particular. All I see is a dreamy blur as I imagine James at the photo lab, leaning on the counter, elbow on the bench, his brown hair falling into his eyes. His masculine hands holding the rolls of film from last night, and his brown jacket resting against his jeans, and his warm thighs.

I feel so aroused just thinking about him. How am I going to cope with having lunch with him tomorrow?

23

I spend the afternoon painting in what I'd describe as a 'lovesome daze'. Very Romantic period, I know. Romantic period and James rolled into one. I love how he's teaching me new things. New words. I feel as though I'm painting with a different stroke. Does that sound weird? And I not only feel his influence on me in terms of how I'm painting, but also in the way I'm thinking. My whole way of experiencing the world feels so different. In a good way.

When I ride in to Harland at five-thirty, I don't notice anything except the cold breeze against my face. I'm much too busy dreaming about James to focus on my surroundings. And when I wheel my bike up from the gutter, and then along the side path, I find myself singing 'Do It Again' by Marilyn Monroe. I know all the lyrics thanks to the *Best of Marilyn Monroe* CD Lucy always plays.

I rest my bike against Dave's, so they're both leaning hard up against the side of the shed. Desperate to tell Dave and Lucy all about last night, I skip up the stairs and push open the back door. Then my confidence dips as Lucy throws her first words towards me: 'Joni, that's going to break if you push it that hard.' Her tone of voice is on the border between harsh and normal. But her light scold dissolves quickly as she tenderly showers me with questions about James. *What happened last night? Do you think you two will get together? Is it Love Love, not God Love?*

While Lucy is sitting with me at the staff table, engrossed in my every word, Dave runs in halfway through my story and begs me to backtrack. I tell them all about the ferry photo, the swings, our favourite poets, James calling me today, tomorrow's planned lunch date. While I'm talking, I flit my eyes back and forth from Dave's greasy chef's face above his stained white shirt to Lucy's red-lipped, flawless, olive-skinned face, and her blonde locks falling onto her pale pink angora cardigan, which of course is low cut and tightly fitted.

Dave revs me up by asking a few questions on the dirty side. We all laugh when I tell them there has been no dirty action. Yet. And they both agree with me when I suggest that the staff dinner is going to be heaps of fun.

Michael calls out a soft 'Hi Joni' from the kitchen, and I note the way Dave doesn't react. Wow. So Michael mustn't have told Dave about him and Annabelle. Otherwise I predict Dave would have mentioned it to me, expressing his immense confusion and surprise over this pairing. Interesting. Maybe Michael won't say anything until the staff dinner.

I wonder whether I should tell Dave about my fight with Annabelle. We've already made up, though, so there's not much point. I decide to leave it. Besides, my news about James is above everyone and everything.

As Dave makes me a coffee, Juliet flumps into the room with a loud sigh. Her hair is out and wet. Freshly washed, probably; she smells strongly of two-dollar strawberry-scented shampoo. She's trying out green eyeshadow tonight, and of course it doesn't suit her one bit. Her fingertips are discoloured from—let me guess—dye, from her resin jewellery. She's in what looks like a red Mrs Claus pantsuit, which makes me wonder whether she's going for a Christmas theme, with the green eyeshadow. The fabric is like fluffy felt. Another outfit from her niece's dress-up box?

And then the complaining begins. Juliet has nothing to wear to the staff dinner. Lucy offers to lend her something, while I begin to think how I can help her out. But . . . no. I don't want to lend her anything of mine, and I can't think how to combine any of her outfits so they'd create anything . . . credible.

'OH, THAT'S IT!' Juliet shouts, as though we're a hundred metres away from her, on an oval. 'I've got it, I've got it! There's a dress in my studio!'

And there she goes again. I know she's just throwing in the word *studio* so she sounds like an artist. Am I too cruel? Perhaps her jewellery-making will improve.

When six-thirty comes around, and the first few diners are seated, I'm certain that the evening appears—to the ordinary bystander—to be a bland, boring, quiet and nothing Monday evening. But, lucky for me, I'm able to remain on autopilot while I'm waitressing. At the same time, I think nonstop about James, and everything that has happened between us, and everything I hope *will* happen between us. I'm on a cloud. I'm *in* a cloud.

I *am* a cloud! Light-headed and so, so ridiculously happy. Nothing could lower my spirits. Absolutely nothing.

I don't hang around for knock-off drinks, purely because I'll have more quality time to dream about James if I go home now. I say my goodbyes, rug up, and ride home thinking about—you got it—James.

Darling Street is hushed and undisturbed. Parked cars line its edges, as streetlights shine down from above. I ride in the centre of the road at a slow pace, my thoughts overtaking me every few metres. *Imagine if James is at my place waiting for me.* I pedal a little harder. *Imagine if he's called me, and there's a message on my machine.* I tilt my bike and turn into my street.

And then my sense of reality re-emerges. He doesn't know where I live, even if he does have my number. As I wheel my bike up onto the footpath, unlatch the gate and peer in, it's just my bungalow I see, all on its lonesome. I hurry inside, glancing at my answering machine as I chuck my backpack on the floor. No message. Just PJs and tea and toast and a bit of telly, and then lying awake in my bed, thinking about how excited I am about tomorrow's lunch date.

I wake slowly, gazing out the little window beside my bed, admiring the morning light filtering through the branches of the gum. The sound of my phone ringing startles me. *Shit!* Is it James? Oh my god, he's calling me again! Before our lunch date? I hobble down the ladder stairs, barely awake, barely with it.

'Hello?'

'Joni! It's me. Annabelle.'

'Oh hi. Shit, I thought you might have been James.'

'No, it's just me. He hasn't called you, has he?' Annabelle asks, sounding hopeful.

'Yes! He called me yesterday!'

'Whaaaat! Joni! Amazing!' Annabelle sounds so happy for me. 'And, and . . .?'

'And we're going out for lunch today!'

'Whaaa? Oh my god, that's such great news. What time is your date?'

I glance over at the clock.

'Shit!!! It's eleven o'clock! I'm meeting him at twelve.'

'Okay. Get ready. You've got heaps of time. But one thing—I left my guitar at your place.'

'I know, I know,' I tell her. 'Sorry. I forgot to tell Michael last night.'

'Oh, no worries. It's actually been nice having a bit of a break from . . . well . . . I feel really relaxed around Michael. Like, I'm not as worried about all my upcoming shows, and my new record deal in the States, and my budget for my next promo tour. All that shit. Michael's so calm and . . . really good for me, I think.'

'It makes me happy hearing that,' I tell her, noting that my prediction about them was spot on.

'Can I come and pick up my guitar tomorrow arvo?

'Yeah sure. Okay, I need to—'

'Yeah. Go, go. You get ready.' Then she says cheekily, 'Don't do anything I wouldn't do.'

'Ha ha,' I say, with a hint of sarcasm.

'Bye, Joni.'

'See ya.'

I take a cup of coffee into the bathroom with me, and prepare for my lunch date. I give myself an extra soaping, and while I dry myself with a towel I ponder how I should wear my hair. Up or out? I decide on leaving it out, so it falls over my shoulders. As I'm slipping into my blue floral dress, I wonder where James is. What is he doing right now? I think about his sensuous lips, his sad, soft brown eyes, his playful nature, his funny observations and his beautiful hands.

I throw on my big navy cardi, and my denim jacket over the top. I look in my full-length mirror for an awfully long time, and then put on some tights and my Blundstone boots. Silver hoop earrings. Sandalwood oil. And then another cup of coffee, after which a rush of nervous anticipation sets in, then doubles, and then triples.

As I head out the gate, the good old butterflies take flight inside my tummy. What will we talk about? What should I say? I try to calm myself down, but it's no use.

24

James pushes his chair out and stands tall. He's wearing a light grey hoodie under a beat-up black leather jacket, and faded blue jeans. His dark-brown hair is in a beautiful mess, and he's slightly unshaven. He reaches out and lovingly puts his arms around me, and I hug him back, but I'm too nervous to absorb how it feels.

'How are you?' he asks, and the sight of his face up close makes me weak at the knees.

'I'm . . . good,' I tell him, taking a seat, watching him sit down again in his own chair. He reaches out for a menu, and I watch his fingers, wishing I could hold them in the palm of my hand.

'Did you get lots of painting done yesterday?' he asks, looking into my eyes with interest.

'Yeah, I did.' I fumble with the knife and fork in front of me. 'Whoops,' I say, as I accidentally knock my knife off the table. How embarrassing. I awkwardly reach down to pick it up, and he smiles, sending me the message that he adores me. At least, that's what I think he's doing. Hope he's doing. 'I'm happy with how this new one's coming along. I was playing around with adding a touch more amber. It's such a fine line, though. One slight variation in colour, and the whole work changes. You know? The mood, the energy. I'm quite obsessed with it.'

'That's beautiful,' he says. 'A beautiful thing, to be that passionate about your work.'

I blush, and hold tight to his compliment.

'How 'bout you? Did you drop the film off okay?'

'Yeah.'

'And then what did you get up to?' I ask, feeling so privileged to be sitting opposite him.

Instead of answering me, he quickly asks, 'Shall we order? I need to head back into the city for a meeting with my agent. I'm so sorry I can't stay too long.'

Oh no, he doesn't want to stay long. Maybe he doesn't like me? Has he invited me here to tell me that he just wants to be friends? Maybe that's all we are anyway? I've built things up too much.

'Yep, let's order,' I agree, hoping my facial expression isn't exposing my paranoid thoughts.

A waitress comes to our table and looks down at James. I can tell she thinks he's hot.

'What would you like, Joni?' James asks me politely.

'Um.' *Fuck. I can't read. Too nervous.* Each line of the menu is a blur.

James waits patiently, then tells the waitress, 'I'll have the lentil burger with chips, thanks.'

'Oh, me too,' I say, and then worry that James will think I have no brain; I just copy what other people do.

The waitress leaves us, and James answers my question.

'So yeah, I dropped the film off. Thank you so much again for suggesting that room for the shoot, Joni.'

We talk more about Harland, and I tell him all the funny things that happened at the summer staff dinner. And then I fill him in on Michael and Annabelle getting together on Sunday night, and how the whole thing was a bit awkward, but I don't go into details.

'So,' he says with a smile, 'I want to know more about you.'

'And I want to know more about you.' I relax, feeling reassured that he's still into me.

'How long have you lived in Balmain?' he asks, pouring me a glass of water from the jug on the table.

'About six months,' I tell him, crossing my legs. 'I like living here,' I add. 'What made you want to move back to Australia? Didn't you like London?'

'I love London,' he says, filling up his own glass. 'I moved over there 'cause I started getting work there, and I hated the long flights. I had some friends from Sydney living there as well, so I knew I wouldn't feel lost in such a big city.'

He smiles at me, and I wonder whether he might reach over and hold my hand, but he doesn't.

'The reason I moved back is because Mum's pretty sick. As soon as I found out she wasn't well, I came back to be with her.'

'Oh no,' I offer gently.

'Mum's . . . she's . . . I have a really close relationship with her. She was already a bit disappointed when I told her I was moving over to London, just because we get on well, and enjoy each other's company. I really love her.'

'Oh, that's so nice.' I feel like I could fall in love with him, especially now that he's telling me how much he loves his mum.

'Yeah.' He pauses, and looks down at the pot plant sitting beside the doorway into the café. 'She has stomach cancer,' he says, and I can tell it's hard for him to talk about it.

'Oh gosh, that's awful. Is she undergoing treatment?'

Our lentil burgers arrive, and James picks up a chip. I watch him put it in his mouth, and I feel all warm and fuzzy between my legs, yet so sad about his mum at the same time. And also bad for feeling turned on at such an inappropriate moment.

'Yeah. She's partway through chemo. That's why I moved back. I wanted to be close to her while she was dealing with . . . It's been pretty rough, but we still manage to laugh and talk about stupid things and . . . Dad's been great.'

I take a bite of my burger, and feel certain that I have tomato sauce all over my face, with iceberg lettuce stuck on. I wipe my mouth, and James gives me the most handsome smile.

'Well, that's really kind of you,' I tell him. 'Leaving your life in London so you could be here with your mum.'

Then we both do some eating, as I think how beautiful it is that James—who obviously moved to London to develop his career as a photographer—moved back home to be by his mum's side in a time of need. What a caring man.

'She only has a few more months of chemo, and then . . . the doctors are saying she has a good chance, so hopefully she'll be fine,' he says before he takes another bite of his burger.

At the same time as I feel honoured that James chose to open up to me about his mother, a sense of disappointment washes over me at the thought of him moving back to London in a few months.

'So do you think—'

'You're about to ask me if I'm going back to London, aren't you?' he says with a cheeky grin.

I shrug, blushing.

'I know you already, Joni. Well, not as well as I'd like to know you.' We both laugh a little, and I lower my gaze to my half-eaten burger. 'I'm having an exhibition here at the end of the year.'

'Oh, great.' I hope desperately that this will mean he's not moving back to London any time soon.

'I still travel quite a bit for work, but now that I've met you, and you live here,' he says, with a flirtatious delivery, 'I'd like to hang out with you some more.'

'That sounds good. I'd like to hang out more with you too,' I confess, returning his mischievous gaze.

I cannot believe this is happening!

We talk some more, and finish our burgers. He tells me he's planning to gather together a bunch of his portraits for his upcoming exhibition, and that he'd love me to visit his studio at The Rocks and have a look through them. They're all pretty large format, and he has a large darkroom, hence his big studio space.

'And I'd still love to come and see some of your paintings,' he tells me, moving his dark-brown hair out of his eyes with a gentle swipe of his hand.

'Well . . .' I fall into a wide grin. 'My studio space is a corner. In my tiny bungalow.'

We both laugh.

'I'm sure it's beautiful.' He stares into my eyes for a long time.

I break the silence at last. 'Are you still coming to the dinner at Harland tomorrow night?'

'Of course,' he tells me, signalling the waitress over, and handing her cash for our meals.

'Oh, let me get it,' I offer.

'You can get the next one.'

Knowing that he wants there to be more James and Joni lunch dates gives me the courage to ask, 'Would you like to come over to my place tomorrow so I can show you some of my paintings?'

'I'd love to, Joni.' He licks his lips with such understated sensuality that I almost pass out.

I pull myself together. 'Maybe four? Does that sound okay? Then we can go to the dinner together.'

'It's a date,' he tells me.

Then he reaches into his bag and pulls out a worn diary. I tell him my address, watching the way his hand moves fluidly across the page as he writes it down. We both stand, and he apologises for needing to leave after such a short time.

'That was really nice,' I tell him.

He puts his arms around me, and I feel very certain that, when we let go of our embrace, we'll kiss. But no! We don't. This is killing me.

'So, four o'clock tomorrow. I really look forward to it, Joni. You're . . . I'm so glad I met you.'

'I feel the same.'

We say goodbye, and I slowly walk away, unable to wipe the smile from my face. As I take a left off Darling Street, I turn my head back towards Café Blue, and catch James climbing onto a bus headed for the city. To me, his catching a bus is even more charming and alluring than a man in a convertible sports car or a boy on a motorbike. And besides, he lives on a boat.

*

When I get back to my bungalow, I potter and paint and lie on the couch, staring up at the wooden-slat ceiling for what would probably be described as an unhealthy amount of time. But I feel overwhelmed by the major crush I've developed on James. He is so dreamy. I am falling for him in such a big way. Hugely and madly. This is so new for me.

At around six I put the kettle on, make a cup of tea, and cosy up close to the heater. It's Tuesday—one of my nights off from working at Harland—so I do my usual, and watch a re-run of *The Golden Girls*. I to and fro between laughing out loud and feeling like a loser for watching such a lightweight show. Then I suddenly panic at the state of my bungalow.

I do a little tidying up, make myself some dinner, and go to bed gazing out through the little box window at the leaves of the gum tree. Tomorrow he's coming here! I—cannot—believe—it!

25

The morning drags, like the long drags Lucy takes on her cigarettes, but in slow motion, and on loop. I can't quite concentrate on getting work done, so I continue with the aimless pottering, while my mind carries on imagining how amazing it's going to be having James here. I go through a few outfit options in my head, pull a few clothes from my rack, then decide that I won't wear a dress. I rearrange the glasses and mugs in my cupboard, clean my bathroom, tidy my clothes rack, neaten my bookshelf, make a vegie soup, and sit out on my verandah.

The day finally makes its way into the afternoon. As I'm checking the clock, noting that it's just after three, Annabelle shows up. I forgot she was coming over to pick up her guitar, but I'm so happy to see her. I serve her up some soup, and we sit together at the table as she devours it. I fill her in on my lunch date with James yesterday. She's excited for me, as I knew she would be.

'He's coming over soon,' I finally tell her.

'What! Here?'

'Yep.'

'Oh my god! Do you want me to go, or . . .'

'No, stay, stay. I'm really nervous about him being here. It'll help having you here too.'

'I'll stay for a bit, but then I'll leave, yeah?'

'Um . . . yeah. Do I look okay? Is this outfit alright?'

Annabelle looks over my light blue jeans and baggy white T-shirt.

'Joni, you look great. Always.'

We move over to the couch and sit together, enjoying each other's company.

'I saw Rebecca on my way in,' Annabelle says. 'Sitting on her back porch. She's so pretty.'

'I know. She's quite perfect, isn't she? And she's so in love with Peter. They're like my mentor couple.'

'Yeah, I get that.'

Annabelle and I chat about Jung's personality types. About our favourite scene in *Pulp Fiction*, and why. And whether Annabelle should dye her hair black, which gets a definite *no* from me. We break out into a fit of laughter after she apologises for her loud sex, then we make a bet on whether James and I do it tonight. Twenty dollars. I say no, she says yes.

Before we know it, we hear the crackle of feet walking over the leaves on the lawn. I look at Annabelle, who pulls a hilariously goofy face: her jaw drops, her eyes widen, and her eyebrows rise higher than I've ever seen them go. My fear melts and I burst out laughing, trying desperately to be as quiet as a mouse.

Next thing we know, James appears in the doorway. He's holding a cardboard box full of oranges.

'Hi,' he says, placing the box down on the doormat. We hug awkwardly, and I savour every second of our clothed bodies touching. His black loose-knit jumper, soft against my white T-shirt, his jeans-covered thighs hard up against mine. My cheek rests on his shoulder for a brief moment, and his beat-up leather jacket feels cold against my skin. We pull back from our embrace.

'I bought these oranges at the market yesterday. I thought you might like some. I have another box in my car. They're amazingly sweet.'

'Thank you,' I say, thinking how adorable he is for bringing me oranges. He picks up the box and hands it to me. Our fingers touch, causing my heart to race as I carry it over to the kitchen table.

'Hi Annabelle,' James says politely.

'Hi James. Thanks so much for taking the photos the other night, and sorry I was . . . I'd had way too much to drink.'

'Oh, no worries. I think the photos are going to come up really well. What a great room Joni suggested for the shoot, hey,' James says. Then he takes in my bungalow.

I watch his gentle eyes look at my crammed bookshelf, the half-finished painting that rests on my easel, my record player, and records leaning against the left-hand speaker, my messy clothes rack with my colourful collection of scarves and second-hand dresses, and the straw hats that hang on each end. His gaze follows the ladder steps up towards my bed on the mezzanine.

Finally he turns to me. 'I love your place, Joni. I love all your things.'

'Thanks,' I tell him, blushing.

I can't handle it. The welcoming chitchat that I normally offer up when someone enters my bungalow is unable to find its way from my brain to my mouth. I'm speechless. All I can do is stare into his eyes, and he's staring back at me.

'Would you like a tea? Coffee?' I finally ask him, fidgeting and playing with my fingers, then tucking both hands in the front pockets of my jeans.

'Tea would be really nice.' He follows me as I move over towards the kettle on the kitchen bench. 'Just tea with milk, if you have it?'

Annabelle picks up a book and pretends she's reading, popping her head up and glancing at us every now and then. After I make James and myself a cup of tea, we stand in the kitchen, and he tells me all about his older sister, Jenny. How she's travelling in Spain, and has become obsessed with flamenco dancing.

'She's learning Spanish, and working in a bar. She was studying for her doctorate in political science, but last year she decided it's not what she wants to do with her life. She's been sending me letters from Madrid, and she sounds so, so much happier. I think it's great she went over there. So many people hang onto these soulless jobs that they hate—the boring nine-to-five slog. I've never wanted that. That's what I love about being a photographer. I travel—sometimes I'm on a shoot on the top of a building at midnight, other times I'll be shooting in the desert.'

I move in towards him, enjoying every word.

'I'm much closer to Jenny than my younger sister Sophie. I've always looked up to Jenny. We have a similar . . . spark, I guess you'd call it. The same things make us tick.'

'So you're a middle child, hey,' I ask him, thinking about my mum's obsession with position in the family. I bring this up with James, and we agree that being an only child is probably the most fortunate position to be in.

'I know,' I tell him. 'When I was little, and I was sick, I remember Mum and Dad both running to me, and smothering me with love and kisses and . . . Mornings would be me jumping into bed with them. I loved that. No other kids around. It was like I was friends with my parents, instead of being their kid.'

'You would have been so cute when you were little,' he says, locking his eyes with mine.

I sit up on the kitchen table, legs dangling off, in an attempt to hide my nervousness. I look over at Annabelle on the couch, and see her peering over the top of the book she's 'reading'. Her eyes shine as she catches me watching her, and I can tell she's smiling behind the pages. James leans against the kitchen bench, telling me about his family. 'Jenny, being the eldest, was always the first to do everything. She went overseas first, moved out of home first, broke a bone first . . .'

'Have you broken anything?'

'Ah, yeah, I was bucked off a horse on a family holiday, in a big paddock next to these falling-down stables.'

'Jesus!'

'I know, it's like, a ye olde accident, isn't it? Jenny had a crash on her motorbike around the same time, and now she has a really cool scar on her arm. Just there.' He runs his finger diagonally across his forearm, then removes his leather jacket and places it softly on the table next to me. I move my eyes over his shoulders and chest, and then he catches me doing it, and I become terribly self-conscious. He smiles, as though he's enjoying me checking him out.

'So what did you break? Arm or leg?'

'I broke my collarbone. Feel this.' He touches his left collarbone. I hop off the table, walk closer to him, and run my fingers over his shoulder. I move my hand down a little lower, and find his collarbone.

'Feel that bump?' he asks.

I feel it.

'Ouch!' he says, making me jump. 'It doesn't really hurt,' he adds quickly. 'Sorry—I was joking. Oh no, you look worried.'

He holds onto my hand, the one that touched him, as if to physically demonstrate his apology. He squeezes it ever so gently, and I turn my palm slowly, until we are properly holding hands.

'I really like you,' he says quietly, coming closer.

I look to see if Annabelle's watching—of course she is— then I look right into James. 'I really like you too.'

'Sorry about that stupid *Ouch*.'

'It was funny. I'm sorry I jumped.'

We let go of each other's hands and he asks if he can see some of my paintings.

'Sure.' I lead him over to my corner set-up.

'I love this one,' he says, standing in front of the painting I'm working on.

'Oh, thanks. I think I was telling you the other night that the theme I'm exploring at the moment is portraying the energy and feelings felt or exchanged between two people.' As I speak, I flash forward to working on a painting of me and him.

'I love that as a concept.' He glances at my open sketchbook. 'Do you mind if I take a look?'

'Of course. They're just ideas I have floating around. I like to sketch things up at random times of the day. Well, some nights. Middle of the night, actually.'

James slowly looks over every inch of every page he turns. 'These are beautiful,' he tells me. 'I love this one.'

He points to a sketch I did of the gum tree in the backyard, viewed from the box window just above my bed.

'I've always been so in awe of people who can paint and draw,' he says, shifting his eyes from my sketchbook to me. 'I can't draw to save my life.'

'Yeah, but I bet your photographs are incredible. I'm hopeless with a camera.'

Before we're able to go any further down the path of complimenting each other, Annabelle announces, 'Well, I should get going, Joni.'

'Oh yeah, yeah.' I look over towards her as she picks up her guitar. 'We'll see you out the gate,' I tell her, wondering if that's awkward with James here, or normal, or whatever. 'You wanna come?' I ask him.

'Sure,' he says, 'but can I look at more of your sketches when we come back inside?"

'Yeah, of course,' I tell him.

James follows me, and the three of us make our way over the lawn. When we reach the gate, Annabelle puts her arm on my shoulder. 'See ya, Joni.'

'See you in a bit, at the dinner,' I tell her, excited about rocking up to Harland with James.

'Yes!' she exclaims. 'Can't wait!'

I close the gate behind her and turn to look at James.

'I never got you that tea. I'll put the kettle on?' I ask him, as we both walk slowly back towards my bungalow.

'That sounds good.'

He puts his hand on my shoulder, and we turn towards each other, then come to a complete stop. Leaning in towards me, he lays a tender kiss on my lips. I kiss him back, feeling inexperienced. We hold hands, and walk up the stairs towards my front door. There's a lightness to my step as I float into the kitchen and fill the kettle. Is this the beginning of my entering into boyfriend territory? For the first time in my life? I think it might be. Although I may be jumping the gun a little.

The kettle clangs as I place it on the hot plate. I look over at James, down on his knees, flipping through my record collection. He pulls out *Slanted and Enchanted* by Pavement.

'Love this,' he says. 'Reminds me of when I lived in London. Oh my god, shooting in this crazy studio, and then one of the big light-stands fell over and missed me by about this much.' He makes a funny face and a tiny pinch with his fingers, looking into the space between his forefinger and thumb. I laugh as I walk over to him.

He slowly gets up and comes towards me, meeting me halfway. His hands feel warm when I reach out for them. Then the sensation of his lips kissing mine for a second time unlocks the gate, and all of my worries are set free. They float up towards the sky, where they dissipate into nothingness, as a sense of contentment rolls in on the breeze.

26

We wander over to the art corner, teacups and saucers in hands, back to where we were before we saw Annabelle to the gate. James flips over another page in the sketchbook he'd been examining, and my milky tea splashes over the edge of the red saucer, onto the floorboards. I rub the sole of my Blundstone boot over it and James gives me a smile, as though approving of my bohemian method of cleaning up spills.

'Wow, this one's amazing,' he tells me. I move in closer to him and look over his shoulder, as he affectionately runs his fingers down my arm. I bring my cup to my lips and take a sip.

'Have you been here?'

'Where?'

'New York. That's the Statue of Liberty isn't it?'

'Yes, it is. Um, yeah, about ten years ago I went on a trip with Mum and Dad. Well . . . Mum was going for her work. We didn't travel all that much. We didn't have much money. But Mum really wanted to visit all the big galleries—MoMA, the Guggenheim. She saved up for quite a few years.'

'So how old were you?'

'About eleven. I loved it. Dad had given me a little Instamatic camera, and I took photos of all the touristy things, like the Statue of Liberty. That's why I sketched it. Not then. A few months ago. I kept all the photos from the trip—look, I have them in this box.'

I place my teacup and saucer on top of the messy shelf where I keep my paints and sketchbooks and art stuff, and pull out a small square cardboard box. I lift the lid and reveal multiple square-format photographs lying in an untidy pile, their corners poking out this way and that. The ones we can see on top are slightly out of focus, and their muted tones obviously appeal to James, because his face lights up.

'Oh, I love these,' he tells me.

'Have a look through.'

James takes one out. 'Is that your mum?' he asks, looking at a photo of Mum standing in front of a yellow taxi in Manhattan.

'Yeah. Look at what she's wearing. She looks hilarious. That hair!'

James smiles. 'She's so pretty.'

He pulls out a few more photos.

'Dad's bookshop,' I explain.

'Wow, I didn't know your dad owned a bookshop. Hang on, I know that one. Is that in Glebe?'

'Yeah. It's still there.'

'I bought this incredible landscape photography book there a few years ago. Before I moved to London.'

'Well, you've probably already met my dad then.'

We smile at each other, and James touches my arm again. He pulls out a few more photos.

'What model camera is this?' he asks. 'I have the 100 and the X-15F.'

'Oh, mine's the . . . I have no idea what model mine is.' I walk over to my bookcase in search of my Instamatic camera and find it nestled on top of my stack of second-hand children's encyclopaedias.

'Oh, it's a 100,' I tell James, touching the cold metal on the face of the camera with my fingertips. I play with the little black wrist strap attached to the side as fond memories fill my mind. I remember being a little girl, in my baby-blue parka, walking across the Brooklyn Bridge and listening to Dad's history lesson on how the bridge was built. Its Neo-Gothic open truss design, the deaths involved during its construction et cetera. Oh, he went on and on, totally in his element, pointing here and there, trying to keep his voice one level higher than all the honking horns and trucks and traffic.

'Here.' I hand my camera over to James, and then I lean in further and kiss him.

This time we kiss for ages. Like a real proper pash, although that makes it sound throwaway. It is anything but. It makes me feel things I've never felt before, and it makes me want more. More James. More of his mind, and more, much more of his body. We stare into each other's eyes.

'A friend of mine had one of these,' he tells me, refraining from taking our kiss to the next level. This is killing me.

'Have it,' I tell him, and this time I affectionately rub the palm of my hand up and down his forearm. I'm trying to send him the message: *We can climb the stairs to my bed and roll around under the covers right now, if you want.*

'No . . . it's yours,' he tells me, as he leans in and kisses me.

This time, he runs his fingers through my hair, and I put my hands around his waist. We pull apart, and I stare into his beautiful brown eyes.

He's under my spell as much as I'm under his. We're under each other's. It's equal. Equal infatuation. Equal adoration.

And then the phone rings and ruins everything.

'Hang on,' I tell him, holding his hand, backing towards the phone, until our arms are stretched out straight between us. I finally let go, so I can get to the phone.

'Hello?' I say.

'Joni? Joni?'

'Oh, hi Lucy.' I look over to James, who is sifting through my box of old photographs. He pulls one out, examines it, and places it on the shelf.

'I've already decorated Gatsby, so there's no need . . .'

'Oh sorry, I said I'd come and help set up.'

'Yeah, yeah,' she says sarcastically, as if she knew I'd forget.

I'm scared she's going to tell me off, so I give her the important information. 'James is here.'

'Oh my god, Joni! Sorry. Am I interrupting? Sorry, love.'

'No,' I lie, and look over to James.

'Well, you two should get your little tushes down here anyway. The dinner has officially started. Juliet's here. Dave's here.'

I glance up at the clock. 'Oh shit, I didn't realise the time. Okay,' I look around my bungalow, and then down at what I'm wearing. 'Sorry, Lucy. We'll be there soon. Is there anything I can—'

'Just tell your boyfriend the party's started,' she says playfully.

'Lucy.'

'What? He is your . . .'

'He's not my . . .' I look over at James, fully aware that he's able to hear everything I'm saying. Lucy and I share a long phone silence. I hear Dave singing loudly in the background, and Juliet carrying on with a super loud, over-the-top falsetto laugh.

'Are you there?' Lucy snaps.

'Yeah, yeah, I'm here. We'll be there soon. We'll head off now.'

The sound of Lucy dramatically slamming the phone down makes me feel excited about heading to Harland. Ah, the drama and delicious decor. I love it.

I walk over towards James. 'People are arriving for the staff dinner. Lucy wants us there. Are you okay if we go soon?'

'Oh sure, yeah, that's fine.' James places the snapshots back in the box. 'Where should I . . .'

'I'll put it away,' I tell him, taking the box from his hands and sliding it back into its spot on the shelf. 'I should get changed.'

'Oh, go ahead.'

He pulls a book out of my bookshelf and sits on the couch reading the blurb on the back. I move over to my clothes rack and hunt through my dresses and coats

Where is it, where is it? Ah ha. I pull out my tight black dress, the one with small red rosebuds printed all over it. This is about as sexy as I go.

I take it over to the bathroom and close the door. I slide my jeans down, pull them over my ankles, and chuck them into the corner. I whip off my T-shirt and fling it on top of my crumpled jeans, slip into my dress and zip it up. Sheesh, this is tight!

Staring into the mirror, I pull a crazy face, an I-can't-believe-this-is-happening-to-me face, followed by an I'm-relaxed-poised-and-calm face—even though that's everything I'm not.

I brush my hair, put on a little make-up—just foundation, eyeliner and some pink lip gloss.

Smothering sandalwood oil on my wrists and neck, I take one last look in the mirror, give myself the okay, and walk back out to James. 'I'm ready when you are,' I tell him.

He turns towards me as he gets up off the couch. 'You look . . . gorgeous.'

I blush, and he takes my hands and kisses me on the lips. Another long one.

'I'm just gonna grab a coat.'

I put on my black velvet coat with the tie around the waist, and do it up tight. Slipping into my gold Mary Janes, I suggest to James, 'Shall we?'

'After you,' he says politely.

Keys? Check. Purse in pocket? Check. I walk out the front door and James follows close behind. I lock up and James asks, 'We walking in?'

'Let's ride. I'll give you a double.'

'That sounds like fun,' he tells me, reaffirming our compatibility. I love someone who's up for doing things thirteen-year-old kids do.

I wheel my bike over towards the gate.

'I'll just get my camera,' James says.

He opens the door on the passenger side of his car, and pulls out his camera. He hoists the strap over his shoulder and joins me up on the footpath.

'Climb on,' I tell him. 'That metal rack on the back will hold you, don't you think?'

'I'm a lot heavier than you,' he says, laughing.

'Yeah, but I want to ride you in. You're my guest.'

I look up into his adorable eyes, and he cradles my face in his hands. He stares right into me, and I know he can see everything: Joni as a child, Joni when she's crying, Joni as a teenager, Joni when she's daydreaming.

'You're beautiful.' He gives me a kiss on my lips as the cool winter air dances between us.

'On ya get,' I tell him.

He climbs on the back, and I clumsily get on the seat. This dress is hopeless for riding a bike. It's hitched right up and the whole world can probably see my underpants, but who cares? I've got James, and James has got me. He puts his arms around my waist, and I attempt to take off.

'Shit!' I'm wobbling all over the place, unable to take us anywhere.

We giggle and laugh and James starts to push his feet along the ground, giving us enough momentum to officially take off.

'Wheee!' he calls out. 'Yay Joni, we can fly, we can fly,' he says, and I laugh like crazy.

'Stop it, I'll crash!'

He holds tighter around my waist, and I bump down a driveway, onto the road, make a left onto Darling Street, and let the hill take us. Past the Emerald, along the bitumen road, on our way to Harland.

James moves one of his hands from my waist down onto my bare thigh. I suddenly feel hot and dizzy, and scared I'll wobble the handlebars and lead us into a disastrous collision. Then I pull myself together and cry out, 'You wanna stay over tonight?'

'What?' James calls out, bringing his arm back up around my waist.

'Do you want to stay over tonight?' I repeat, as the sandstone cottages flash past us.

'Joni, that would be . . .'

'What?' I call out, unable to hear what he's saying.

'Yes! Yes!' he yells at the top of his lungs.

I take my left hand off the handlebars and hold onto his hands, wrapped around my tummy. He puts one of his hands on top of mine, the other underneath, making a little hand sandwich.

This is the best day of my life. This is the best day of my life.

We sink down into the valley and, before I even attempt to pedal uphill, I make the call. 'Okay, we ain't gonna be—'

The bike wobbles and we both fall off.

'Ouuuch,' I call out in between bursts of laugher. 'My knee. Owwy.'

'Oh Joni, you've grazed it,' James says, through his giggles.

'It's okay, it's okay,' I tell him, pulling my dress down, and giving my knee a quick wipe as our laughing fit continues.

I take hold of the handlebars and we pull ourselves together and walk up the hill. James puts his arm around my shoulder, and I tilt my head and nestle into his chest, still managing to wheel my bike. When we get to the top, there's Harland, with a big sign on the front door: PRIVATE FUNCTION.

'Come on,' I tell James. 'This way.'

I lead him down the side path, and rest my bike against the shed. I place my cold hand in his, and give him a quick kiss on his lips. Together we climb the stairs to the verandah, and walk in through the back door.

27

The sound of Josephine Baker's voice on the stereo weaves its way through the cozy Bar Room. I head for the hatstand in the corner, and James follows. We remove our coats, and I hang them both, James giving me a quick 'Thanks', along with a little kiss on my lips.

I lead him by the hand over towards the hallway. Dave, wearing a red flannelette shirt over blue jeans, bounces past Lillibon, heading straight towards us. His greeting, as always, is sprightly.

'Joni J!' he calls out loudly.

'Hey Dave.'

'How are ya, mate. Hey James.'

James and Dave man-shake, their faces both showcasing friendly smiles.

'Wait till you see what Lucy's done with Gatsby,' Dave excitedly tells us. 'Babe, babe!' he calls out towards Gatsby. 'Can I bring 'em in? It's Joni.'

'Yeah, yeah yeah!' Lucy frantically calls back, sounding very much like she's in a tizzy.

The three of us walk along the hallway, pausing when we reach the doorway to Gatsby. I look inside, and my mind is blown. Lucy's in the corner, setting up the gramophone on a table covered in a hot-pink tablecloth, with a bright-blue ribboned edging. She wiggles her curvy bum as she fiddles around with the records and the vase of red roses next to the gramophone. Then she turns to face us, wearing her natural resting face: seductive scowl. She looks sexed-up and on fire, and I'm captivated by her electrifying beauty.

Her long blonde hair is out, wavy and full of life. One side is pinned up, held in place with a gold comb covered in white feathers that billow up high above her head. Her thick fringe rests just above her elegantly shaped eyebrows, and large gold hoop earrings hang beside her petite neck. Tiny gold beads and sequins cover her tight, off-white satin dress, its neckline plunging deeply, drawing attention to her voluptuous, olive-skinned breasts. Her lips are a deep red, and her eyes have extra black eyeliner and a thick coat of mascara. Her look is Hollywood Movie Star From Yesteryear meets Parisian Showgirl meets Exotic Bird.

And the room! Lucy's decorated it so it looks like we're about to take part in a pagan wedding ceremony, circa 1924. Gone are all the tables and chairs. Instead, hanging high above, are wide, lollipop-coloured ribbons, each one attached to the lightshade in the centre of the ceiling; from there they stretch out, evenly spaced and pinned three-quarters of the way up the walls, creating a flamboyant canopy.

'It's a maypole,' Lucy tells us, followed quickly by, 'and *bonsoir*, my darlings.'

She gives me a kiss-kiss, and then moves on to James.

'Oh my god, Lucy,' I exclaim, 'this looks amazing!'

I turn to James, whose body language suggests that he's just as enthralled as I am. He takes the lens cap off his camera. 'You two,' he says, gently putting his hand on my back, suggesting I move into the centre of the room.

I sidle up next to Lucy and she swings her arm around my shoulder, pulling a sultry pose for the camera.

'Under the lightshade. It'll look great if you're both under the centre of the maypole,' James tells us, looking ridiculously handsome.

'Oooh, photo time, photo time!' Juliet sings out like a sick parrot, entering the room with an overly exaggerated whoosh.

She squishes herself between Lucy and me without an invitation. 'Move over, girlies,' she orders, boom-booming her hips from side to side.

'Say cheese!' James calls out from behind his camera.

'Whippeee!' Juliet calls out, as Lucy and I obey James, giving him a playful *cheese*.

Juliet's silver-and-black lamé dress almost looks cool. But her big, blow-dried hairdo takes over, destroying every inch of credibility. Meanwhile, her fuzzy peach perfume overtakes every other fragrance in the room. I look towards her and smile lovingly, enjoying the entertainment she unknowingly provides.

'Juliet, do you remember James from the other night—the photographer?' Lucy asks, her French accent sounding so obvious on *photographer*.

'I don't know if I properly met you, but howdy. I'm Juliet.'

She shakes his hand, up and down, up and down, so fast it sets James off with the giggles. I join in, and then put my arm around him, cuddling in, making it obvious to Juliet that he's mine, and I'm his.

'Bubbles?' Juliet asks, flicking her hair across her forehead, then zhoozhing it up at the back, unaware that it's impossible to make it any bigger than it already is.

'Ah, yeah . . . sure,' James answers, in his cool, mellow tone. 'Joni?'

'Yeah, thanks, Juliet.'

'*Oui*,' Lucy purrs, before calling out, 'Davey, baby, how's the food coming along?'

Juliet flits out of Gatsby, and Dave jumps in. He gathers me, James and Lucy together and whispers, 'The caterers don't seem very experienced. Lucy, um . . . where did you find them?'

'*Mais si, ils sont expérimentés!*'

'Babe,' Dave answers Lucy, in his normal voice, 'translate, translate. Joni and James don't speak French. Unless you do, James. Do—'

Lucy fires back at Dave, 'They are professionals, and I found them in the city a few months ago when I was attending a private auction. They are brilliant! How dare you judge my choices, darling.' She cosies up to him and gives him a big smooch on the lips.

A loud knock rattles on the front door. Polly's Pommy 'Hello' is just audible. We hear her let herself in, then she joins us in Gatsby.

'Hello lovelies,' Polly says, holding up a bottle of bubbly.

'*Bonsoir* my love,' Lucy says, gently laying her lips on each of Polly's cheeks, then tossing her long hair over her shoulder.

Juliet appears with a silver tray of coupes, each one filled with champagne.

'Polly, did you meet Juliet?' Lucy asks, as Juliet leans over Lucy's shoulder. I watch Juliet give Polly the once-over as Polly removes her leopard-print coat, revealing a fabulous sapphire-blue strapless dress. Multiple strands of pink and blue beads are wrapped around her neck, and her dark-brown hair is windblown and messy, adding a paradoxically punk element to her school-prom get-up. When she smiles, somehow her bucked teeth add even more credibility and spunk to her overall appearance. *Look and learn, Juliet*, I think, silently. *Look—and—learn.*

'Hello Juliet,' Polly chirps, then quickly adds, 'Jamie darling!' and gives him a hug. She looks at me and I can tell she's forgotten my name. 'And hello . . .'

'Joni,' James says, saving her.

He pulls me close and puts his arm around my waist, cuddling me affectionately. Polly immediately picks up on the romantic vibe and raises her eyebrows at James, thinking I'm not looking.

We all grab a champagne glass and raise it. 'Cheers,' Lucy says, her delicate hand holding her coupe up high.

Her gold bangles chinkle together as we all answer her call. 'Cheers!'

We mingle, splitting off into twos, talking about this and that. I overhear Polly and James chatting.

'These ribbons look like a bit of alright,' Polly tells James. 'And you look like you've had a good day,' she says to him, with a mischievous inflection.

I look over at them, and she has a twinkle in her eye.

'I've had a very good day. Very, very good.' James looks back at me, his gaze reaffirming his desire for me.

He and Polly clink glasses, then James leaves her standing there and walks towards me. He kisses me, and I feel the weight of everybody's gaze. And then the thick stench of marijuana walks into the room with Simon.

Dave breaks from his conversation with Lucy. 'Simey boy,' he calls, giving Simon a slap/hug across his shoulders.

'Hey mate,' Simon returns, his slurred speech, bloodshot eyes and slow-motion movements revealing his doped-up state just as much as if he had the words *I'M STONED* tattooed across his forehead.

'Where's Annabelle?' Polly calls out, as though she's asking everyone in the room.

'Oh, yeah,' I reply. 'Um . . . she's coming with Michael.'

'Say what?' Dave's wearing his hilarious one-eyebrow-up face.

'Yeah. You'll see,' I tell him, unable to hide my grin.

Lucy moves us into the Red Room, where the dark, wooden walls and red vases and urns and Valentine's Day cards are lit with the golden glow of five candles in a brass candelabra that she's set on the mantelpiece. Six tealight candles are set in a row down the centre of the table, and stemless red roses are scattered over the delicate mismatched china and white napkins. The fireplace is bursting with flickering flames atop blackened logs with hot fiery coals. We all take a seat, James and I making sure we're seated side by side. Once we've sat down and tucked our chairs under, James places his hand on my thigh. He looks me in the eyes and I return his gaze, thinking back to Sunday night, when I first saw him. I can't believe this is where we are now.

'Some wine?' Lucy asks, pouring chablis into Polly's glass, then moving on to Juliet's.

Annabelle's voice floats from the hallway into the Red Room.

'Hello people.'

Michael appears in the doorway, and half a second later Annabelle pokes her head over his shoulder, then slips in beside him. She's wearing a beautiful baby-blue silk dress with shoe-string straps, red lipstick, and a black velvet choker. I give her a smile, admiring the way her diamante earrings are catching the candlelight. She strokes the side of Michael's face, making it very obvious that they are on, as a couple.

'Sorry we're late,' she says, directing her apology to Lucy.

Lucy gives them both the up-and-down, and I study her face, wondering which way she'll go. Pissed off and snappy, or warm and delighted to see that Michael has scored one of the most gorgeous up-and-coming superstars in the country.

'*Bonsoir,* darlings,' she purrs, waltzing up to Annabelle and giving her the double-kiss greeting, followed by a friendly rub on Michael's back.

'Hey Michael,' Dave says, raising his wine glass and giving him a cheers with eyebrows suggestively bopping up and down.

Polly moves along so she can sit next to Annabelle, and Annabelle can sit next to Michael; the room quickly fills with effervescent conversation and jovial chitchat.

When the two caterers enter the room with our entrées, I realise how lucky we are at Harland, not having to wear a white lab coat waitressing uniform, or the standard black-and-white. Not with Lucy as our boss. That would be very un-Harland.

The food is delicious, the wine is flowing, and the mood is developing from standard-dinner-party to raucous share-house get-together. Before the dessert is served, we're already razzed up enough to spill into Gatsby and crank up the gramophone.

'Okay, music, music . . . Dave, turn the CD player off,' Lucy sternly orders, sounding slightly drunk, and very wound up.

Dave, in loud conversation with Polly, is oblivious to her request.

'*Dave!*' Lucy howls, in her fierce lady-boss voice.

'Yeah, yeah.' He hurriedly pushes past everybody, tapping her on the bum on his way out into the hallway.

Lucy picks up the pile of old records, and dramatically flips through them, dropping one, which lands with a violent slap on the floor. 'Michael,' she snaps, 'wind her up, would you.'

'Ooh la la,' Polly says in half-sing half-talk.

Michael follows Lucy's order and winds up the gramophone.

'I've never seen a real gramophone. Isn't that crazy?' Annabelle rubs Michael on his back, peering over his shoulder. 'Look at it. It's gorgeous.'

Dave re-enters Gatsby, holding a silver tray upon which he's balancing a bottle of port with ornate glasses in a circle around it. 'Babe,' he says affectionately to Lucy.

She swiftly opens the port bottle with a corky pop, and fills all the glasses. 'Anyone?'

'Port?' Polly questions, as though it's the most ridiculous idea she's ever heard of.

Lucy gives her a provocative, sexy look. Polly softens. 'Well, why not?'

James whispers in my ear, 'I hate port.'

'Me too,' I tell him. 'Too sweet.'

We give each other a cheers with our half-full wine glasses, and I snuggle into him. He holds me close and gently rubs the back of my head, playing with my hair. Lucy drinks her port. Dave gives a big 'Whooo!' And then we're off, dancing like a bunch of lunatics to 'Puttin' on the Ritz'.

Juliet and Polly wiggle their bums in time to the music,

chinking their port glasses together, exchanging silly giggles. Dave attempts to dance with Lucy, but she teasingly flits across to the other side of the room and makes a futile attempt to invite Simon onto the dance floor. Annabelle and Michael adopt a cute ballroom dancing embrace as they laugh and whisper in each other's ears. And James embodies the persona of a cabaret performer and sings along, as though he's on a stage.

He sets the room alight with laughter. Then he dives into my arms, kisses me on my neck, and puts one arm around my waist. We give Annabelle and Michael a run for their money, dancing together like a high-society couple at a 1930s soiree. My tummy and boobs hard up against his chest, my arm wrapped around him, my hand just above his bum. The room is filled with electricity and madness, and everyone is having the time of their lives.

28

Eight songs in, I'm starting to feel pooped, coupled with wanting to be alone with James.

'Shall we . . .'

'Yeah, let's go.' James sounds as eager to leave as I am.

'We're going to head off,' I tell Lucy, holding James's hand, wobbling from side to side. I'm slightly tipsy.

Lucy winks, and embraces me. 'Bye love. You two have fun tonight.'

I hand out goodbyes to everyone else, and James does the same, embracing Polly for a long moment, knowing he won't see her again until he's next in London.

I give Annabelle a hug, and she whispers a slurred message in my ear. 'I'm so happy for you.'

I hug her tighter, and then Polly whisks her away from me, the two of them slipping into a cute foxtrot.

I take James by the hand and lead him to the back door. We grab our coats off the hatstand, James swings his camera strap over his shoulder, and we brave the cold night air. The soles of our shoes kiss the wooden steps, and we hold hands all the way down. I collect my bike and wheel it along the side path. James follows, and we walk and wheel the whole way back to my place.

When we arrive at my bungalow, we are well and truly all over each other. I fill two glasses of water in the kitchen and, after we've both taken a sip, we hold each other, kissing passionately. And then I lead James up the ladder steps, onto my bed, where we rest our heads on the pillows. James tells me his funny falling-off-the-top-bunk-at-school-camp story, and I burst out laughing. And then . . . silence.

'This is great, up here,' James finally says, rolling over to look out the small square window. He rubs my leg, and pulls me over, closer towards him. We roll around kissing, and he slowly undresses me. Then he takes off his black jumper and T-shirt. I undo his belt, and he slides his jeans down.

We burst into a fit of laughter when he attempts to pull his jeans over his feet. He sits up and almost bumps his head on the wood-slat ceiling. Once he's kicked his jeans off, he gently climbs on top of me, and kisses my lips, and his kisses are warm and tender.

So this is what making love feels like. This is what truly connecting with someone who adores you feels like. Oh, whoa, hang on, *this* is what it feels like, I think, after he's wriggled his hand into my undies and touched me. I become so excited and wet, I don't know what to do with myself.

'Just let me get a condom,' he says, kneeling upright, and this time he does bump his head on the ceiling. 'Ouch!'

We both laugh. I can't help but look at his wiener pushing out hard from inside his white Calvin Klein undies. I'm dying. Absolutely dying, and ready for it.

'I put one in my pocket,' he whispers, 'because I was hoping . . . I was hoping this might happen tonight.'

'Me too,' I tell him.

And once his undies are off and the condom is on, we have hot, dreamy sex. Our minds and bodies are entwined and so close to each other. So close we become one.

When we're done, we lie naked, side by side, staring up at the wooden ceiling. I turn to the little square window, and watch the branches of the gum tree swaying slowly from side to side.

'You're so gorgeous, Joni.' James rolls towards me and gives me a kiss. 'I love everything about you. I just wanna—I just wanna be with you . . . always.'

'I have the same feeling,' I tell him, pulling the doona up over us, snuggling into him.

'I have to go to New York in a couple of weeks. I need to be there for about a month. Will you come with me?'

'Um, yes, yes,' I answer, so excited that he wants me by his side. 'Oh, but I don't have enough money at the moment to buy a . . . to buy a ticket for the plane.'

'My shout, Joni. I have enough. I want you to come.' He kisses me again, and looks longingly into my eyes. 'Will you?'

I'm suddenly struck with a thought, as though an arrow, launched from the reality bow, has delivered me a bout of doubt. I worry that I'm a weak hanger-on-er. A girl with no strength, no ability to do things on her own.

But I know I'm not that. I know I'm strong and independent. I know what Annabelle says of me is true. And besides, I've dreamed of travelling, and being based in different cities. It would be so inspiring for my art practice. Lucy would give me a month off, I'm sure she would.

I float back into the moment. 'Yes . . . yes. I wanna come.' I kiss James hard. And then I pull back. 'But I'd want to do my own thing too. I'd want to paint, and . . . Does this sound terrible? I want to be my own person. Not just tag along with you. I love being with you so much, but I need my own time. Time to work on my art. I couldn't just be . . .'

'Oh my god, of course. That's why I'm so drawn to you. Your focus on your own art practice. Your beautiful mind, and the way you interpret the world, and then express that through your paintings and drawings. You're a strong independent woman, Joni.'

I smile.

'I wouldn't want to have a girlfriend tagging along with me with nothing of her own going on. I've got some friends in Brooklyn, and I know you could sublet a studio space while we're there, and, you know . . .'

Hang on, he just called me his girlfriend. Didn't he? I know this'll sound embarrassing, but I decide to ask him anyway. 'Will you be my boyfriend, James? I think I might be . . . falling in love with you.'

He runs his palm along the side of my face. 'Of course I'll be your boyfriend. I've been your boyfriend since the night we met, haven't I?'

'Yeah,' I tell him.

We kiss again, snuggle tighter, and eventually drift off to sleep.

*

I wake to the feeling of James kissing my cheek. 'Good morning,' he half whispers.

I kiss him on the lips. It's freezing, so I roll in closer. He's so warm. Like my own personal heater. The light streaming in through the square window beside the bed is bright, as though it's possibly mid-morning.

'Shit, what time is it?' I pull myself up and look down towards the clock in the kitchen. 'It's ten-thirty! I told Lucy I'd help her clean up. I'm supposed to be there now.'

James kisses me again. 'You'd better go then, hey.'

'Can I make you some coffee before you go? And a shower?'

James jumps in the shower while I put coffee on the stove. He walks out of the bathroom, wearing the same outfit he had on last night. We play swapsies—James takes over pouring our coffees, and I have a hot shower, closing my eyes and letting the warm water run all over my face for an extra long time. James looks over at me while I get into jeans and a T-shirt.

'Would you like to come and have lunch with me on my boat today?' he asks me. 'I can drop you back in for work tonight.'

I walk up to him and put my arms around his waist. 'Tonight's my night off. I could . . .'

'Come and have lunch and stay over?' he asks. 'It's small, and—'

I kiss him on the lips. 'I'd love to. I'd love to.'

We kiss again for a long time, and I lean into his lovely body, holding him tight. 'You can hang out here while I help Lucy pack up. The Sunday paper is over there. Does that sound . . .'

'Perfect,' he says.

'I'll only be an hour or so.'

I finish my coffee, clean my teeth, and cuddle in next to

James on the couch for a moment. He's already completely at home, tucked in under the crocheted blanket, flipping through the paper.

'Bye,' I tell him.

We kiss, and kiss again. He holds my hand, and I slowly walk away, until it's just the tips of our fingers touching.

'See you in a bit,' I say, as I step out on the front verandah and close the door.

On my bike, riding down Darling Street, I take in all the familiar sights. Sandstone cottages, Victorian windows, leafless wisteria vines, all flashing by. My heart beats, and it's a love beat. Louder than the sound of the car that overtakes me. Louder than the sound of my breath as I pedal up the hill. James, James. James. Hang on, I don't even know his surname.

I think back to the day after I lost my virginity and laugh out loud, my hair flying in the breeze. My gravestone. If I died today, I know what it would have inscribed on it, and it makes me smile, and it makes me feel full to the brim.

Joni Johnson, aged 21

Died after having hot, dreamy sex with her beloved boyfriend James (surname unknown).

Acknowledgements

Thank you to Annette Barlow, Genevieve Buzo, Hilary Reynolds, Rebecca Allen, Sarah Baker and everyone at Allen & Unwin. I'd also like to thank Eve Nachin for talking with me about all things French, Susanna Hoffs for igniting the spark, Holly Throsby for fueling the fire with her words of encouragement, Darren and Judy for all their love, Lara Meyerratken, Sarah Scheller and my friends and family.

Extra special thanks to Richard Walsh for his support and guidance.

Lastly, I'd like to acknowledge John Keats, as the first few lines of his poem 'Ode to a Nightingale' (1819) are recited by both Joni and James when they are on the swings.

About the author

Sally Seltmann is the award-winning Australian singer-songwriter behind the intoxicating albums *Hey Daydreamer, Heart That's Pounding, Somewhere, Anywhere,* and *The Last Beautiful Day.* She is the co-writer of the hit song '1234', performed by Feist. She previously went under the stage name New Buffalo, and is a member of Seeker Lover Keeper, along with fellow Australians Sarah Blasko and Holly Throsby. Sally is currently working on a new solo album. This is her first book.